Cowards

Cowards

Trent Portigal

**TOP HAT
BOOKS**

Winchester, UK
Washington, USA

First published by Top Hat Books, 2015
Top Hat Books is an imprint of John Hunt Publishing Ltd., Laurel House, Station Approach, Alresford, Hants, SO24 9JH, UK
office1@jhpbooks.net
www.johnhuntpublishing.com

For distributor details and how to order please visit the 'Ordering' section on our website.

Text copyright: Trent Portigal 2014

ISBN: 978 1 78535 070 2
Library of Congress Control Number: 2015932904

A CIP catalogue record for this book is available from the British Library.

Design: Stuart Davies

Printed and bound by CPI Group (UK) Ltd, Croydon, CR0 4YY, UK

We operate a distinctive and ethical publishing philosophy in all areas of our business, from our global network of authors to production and worldwide distribution.

Chapter 1

"People would prefer a railroad; the telephone is very nice but it won't haul wheat," Claude declares.

"We already have railways. We're on a train right now," Lora replies.

"Our own railroads, not those controlled by the Committee."

Dismayed to be sitting across from someone lacking the common decency to avoid contentious topics in public, Lora pretends to not have heard Claude's last words. She looks away, out the window across the uniform grey-brown fields cut regularly by sandy brown range roads. The occasional copse of trees marking the location of farmhouses and silos makes the rest of the landscape seem even emptier. *There is nothing here*, she thinks.

Claude, realizing the reason for her silence, laughs: "The Committee doesn't have much pull on the prairies. They can't afford it. They just do enough to screw things up at the periphery, keep us boxed in."

The fields dissolve in Lora's mind's eye into a uniform concrete grey, the grey of the station platform left behind several hours before. Léon stood straight, a confident, hopeful smile on his face, turning slowly, stiffly to watch his wife disappear. A caricature of strength. He kept his hands in his pockets; it was not the moment for goodbyes. Suddenly he was gone; the train was lost, crawling through tunnels and trenches with regularly spaced platforms emerging momentarily from the subterranean twilight. Occasional glimpses of neighborhoods – residential blending into industrial – offered a tenuous link to the outside world. Then, the train emerged into rolling aspen parkland and the engineer accelerated.

"It's too bad you weren't coming out in the wintertime. The trains are full of hockey teams. Rutting season, we call it, a total lark."

Lora slowly pulls herself back to the present to encourage the new topic: "You play?"

"Yeah, in the too old to take the hits yet too stupid to get off the horse league. We won the 'B' side! Proving that anyone can succeed if expectations are low enough! The only pain felt that day was by other passengers on the train home, listening to us sing. Old patriotic songs; for one day we were actually patriots. The day after, lying in bed trying not to move to avoid the agony, I had my usual epiphany; that I should take up competitive snowball rolling or some such, far more my speed.

"If you stick around long enough, you should come to a game."

"If I stick around long enough?"

"Most folks come from someplace else – it is the frontier after all. But then, most folks don't make it. In the early days, they died, usually in wintertime. It was the isolation, mostly. Groups of volunteers would go around to the new homesteads in the spring, before seeding. Now, with the roads built and kept in decent shape, people just pick up and leave."

"If the problem is the isolation, why don't people just visit each other more? Isn't that why you play hockey?"

"That helps, but it's not enough when your closest neighbor is a couple of kilometers away. Still, you are staying in Kralovna, no?"

"Yes."

"So who knows? It's a sleepy town, maybe you'll like it after the bustle of the capital."

"Maybe. Why would it matter, though? It is the role that has been assigned to me."

"You had no choice in the matter?"

"What a strange question. Why would I? It's not as if I know where I would be the most useful."

"And you think the Committee does?"

"As best they can, yes. You talk about isolation being a major issue. The Committee obviously sees it the same way. Telephones should help better connect people. In the capital, I had no idea that was a problem out here. It would never have crossed my mind. But the Committee did know and here I am."

"Do you have any experience with telephones?"

"No, not very many people do."

"You know, they tried to do the same thing with farming once. The need for farmers is obvious, puts food on the table. So they assigned people with no experience, city folk who didn't quite fit in in the capital. What a disaster. The number of suicides that winter…"

"And the people working for the railways, I imagine?"

"No, that's different. They're straight up underhanded and corrupt. I wish they were just inexperienced."

Lora turns her gaze once more out the window, to fields that seem completely unchanged. She imagines her husband, shoulders slumped from the moment the train was out of sight, walking down the stairs into the station, essentially a passage under the platforms with ticket booths and a café off to one side. She sees him checking his watch, conscious that he will be alone for the foreseeable future, that their children will only have him to rely on. Emerging from the passage, he will have passed shop owners raising the grills and preparing for the morning crowd. He will have created a checklist for getting the kids off to school and then have worked at once more raising his shoulders and finding his smile.

Common decency, perhaps it is only common in the capital. Kralovna could be full of people who have nothing to lose in cursing the Committee and the railways. That would make her life complicated.

Claude takes a more conciliatory tone: "Regardless, you are right, one can't expect workers with much experience with a new invention."

"You don't even know what I will be doing."

"What will you be doing?"

"I don't really know to be honest, but it will be in the main yard. I can't imagine that the technology would make much of a difference in how the place is run. Stuff comes in, is stored, and then goes out. What comes in and goes out is counted so that there is enough – neither too little, nor too much – stock. It doesn't seem complicated."

"Perhaps. I remember when people started to use harvesters with engines. Before then, it was the same old machine. If one was worn down beyond repair, the farmer would buy a new one that was pretty much identical. After, though, he would have to keep track of changes and improvements, figure out what new tools and parts he would need; it all became very complicated. It's great now, but the transition was hard and just because most of us are used to the new machines doesn't mean that they are simple."

"That's strange. Wouldn't all the details be sorted out centrally?"

Claude smiles: "Do you really want an answer? We might as well skip to the silence and looking out the window."

Lora's face reddens. "No, I suppose not."

Silence overcomes them in any case.

Lora pulls the *Letters of Pliny the Younger* from her bag. She contemplates the book for a moment, then places it in her lap, unopened. Léon gave it to her yesterday, their final day together for quite a while, with the letter Pliny sent to Nepos regarding the courage of Arria dog eared. They were sitting together at the kitchen table, no words left to share after months of off and on planning, simply savoring a moment in each other's company with the sounds of the kids horsing around in the background. A plea to Chronos or Saturn or the Committee – whoever controlled the flow of time these days – to eternalize the moment floated in the air, unarticulated. Then, abruptly, Léon left the kitchen, returning a moment later with the *Letters* in hand. "For your trip" was the extent of the explanation as he gave her the book. It was just as well. Situations generally became more confused when he tried to find the logic behind his impulses. Lora found that it made more sense to give her own meaning to these acts, meaning that tended to be closer to the truth than anything he might say.

Arria was famous in ancient Rome for uttering the phrase "Paetus, it does not hurt" after stabbing herself with a knife, showing her husband how to die with courage. Paetus played a major role in a failed coup against the Emperor Claudius and was subsequently ordered by Claudius to commit suicide. He sat, knife in hand, wavering, until his wife took the blade. After hearing her words, he followed her example without hesitation. The letter did not glorify this event, but rather recounted other scenes where, according to Pliny, Arria acted with more courage, concluding "that the noblest words and deeds are not always the most famous."

The letter was ingrained in Lora's mind by the time she boarded the train, but the significance for her remains unclear. She certainly does not feel like Arria, following orders that separate her from her children and husband, shying away from criticizing the Committee, working what will very likely be a meaningless job and, at the heart of it all, accepting the current state of affairs. On this train, heading to what appears to be the middle of nowhere, common decency seems more like cowardice. But does complaining about the railways really change things? Is Claude's futile hostility really better than Léon's forced smile?

Chapter 2

Léon sighs in relief the moment the train is gone. He checks his watch and decides that there is time to stop by the café before seeing the kids off to school. He exits the station to the east and makes his way through a maze of nondescript buildings to a low-key commercial street. Entering the Union Café, a reincarnation of an homage of a half forgotten haunt of poets and writers, he pauses to contemplate the tables, almost all of them empty this early in the morning.

"Lemon tea," he whispers to himself, "what table goes with today's lemon tea?"

He slowly circles the tables, all of them covered in writing. The owner, Hervé, had been inspired to encourage drawing on the tables after watching a scene in a film where a character sketches the beautiful woman he is discussing with his friends on the table where they are sitting and one of the friends immediately asks the proprietor if he can buy the table. One of Hervé's greatest dreams is to replay this scene in his café, in order to shore up his flagging belief that life imitates art.

Unfortunately for him, it was not to be. The first problem was that the place was already overrun with writers and poets, who shunned artists for their incapacity to reflect the incessant movement of modern life in their work. They enthusiastically took Hervé up on his offer to deface the tables, and spent the next several months coming up with a theme. They didn't want to write about anything of importance, anything that had a real connection to them or their aesthetic predilections. This was largely because, while they didn't mind being hauled off for writing something deemed inappropriate, the police did not have the good graces to allow them to finish their drink before taking them in, which undermined one of the main reasons to frequent the café in the first place. So, after due reflection, they decided that the limited real estate made poetry the obvious form and that all of it was to be a take on the lines:

Once again I see
These hedge-rows, hardly hedge-rows, little lines
Of sportive wood run wild

The lines could have inspired some interesting verse, had the regulars the vocabulary and experience to express nature or felt some visceral pull to romanticism. As it was, the words written resembled learning aides for children who were getting to know the species of trees and birds for the first time: amusing yet superficial and safe. This is to say that, from the poets' point of view, the experience was a great success. Hervé on the other hand was morose for quite some time afterwards, grumbling that as soon as he had the money he would replace the tabletops and find a more refined clientele.

Then the caprices of the Committee struck, eager as they were to ensure that the local wordsmiths were saying the right things. One morning, lost amongst his cinematic fantasies, Hervé opened the café to find a room filled only with chairs.

Falling into the chair closest to the door, he blurted out, "They were beautiful after all, sublime, I just couldn't see it!"

The shock of the missing tables melded with his dreams, creating a bizarre scenario involving international thieves and black markets. He decided after a moment that he didn't really like the scenario of his tables being whisked off in the dark of night to be added to the private collection of some rich foreigner; he actually liked his tables and considered them part of the ambiance of the establishment. In any case, the response in the film to the request to buy the table was a firm 'no'.

Later that day, reality set in when two inspectors took him for a cup of coffee. He was taken to a warehouse on the other side of town. Inside, he found his tables placed neatly in rows on the bare concrete floor. Over the next week, Hervé and the two inspectors sat at each table, where they followed a well-worn pattern. First, one of the officers would offer him a coffee. He accepted for the first table in the morning and the first in the afternoon, and refused politely after that. Then, the interrogators took turns asking him the same question in regards to each poem written on the table: "What is your opinion of how this writing furthers the slanderous campaign against our country?" He would invariably answer "I refuse to testify" in a soft, almost apologetic voice. This would continue for the standard working day, at which point they drove him back to his café. At the end of each day, he would ask "When will you return my tables to me?" to which the reply was always "Don't confuse the issue."

The next week, the tables were back and Hervé was in a far better mood. He decided that a dash of originality was a good thing and dreamed of a day when someone would pay homage to his tables in their own café. Every year, he would spend a week or two in the warehouse, following the same pattern. It was a way to remind those who didn't want to be of interest to the police that it would likely be better to frequent a different establishment, and to discourage the congregation of certain people at inconvenient times.

Léon decides that the conifer table by the window overlooking the side street will suite today's lemon tea nicely. He sits and calls out his order to Hervé, perched behind the counter either lost in whatever fantasy has taken his fancy this morning or simply dozing. Hervé snaps back to reality, prepares the infusion and carries over the small pot and cup. He then sits down at the table and gazes out the window.

Léon starts talking, half to himself: "Sure, the mutual suicide of Arria and Paetus is a bit grim, and the bit about supporting the death of her daughter, also grim."

Hervé nods, having no idea what Léon is talking about and in any case not really listening.

Once the tea is sufficiently over-steeped for Léon's taste, he pours himself a cup and continues: "The question is whether it is obscure enough to distract her for seven hours."

"I wonder what I would need to do to get more young people in here."

"What are you saying, Hervé? This rose has not lost its bloom."

"Besides us and the government, nobody knows that the conifer table exists. And, everyone knows what the three black cars parked across the street mean. Okay, yes, the table is not necessarily the pinnacle of poetic achievement. Still, the only people who come here are those who have already gone for a cup of coffee with the police. For the rest, the risk isn't worth it, but how do they know if they don't know what's in here? Will everything we've done be lost to creative types just starting out?"

"The journal gets around."

"How do you know? Do you talk to people, I mean other people?"

"I look in trash bins sometimes."

"Toilet stalls?"

"Those too."

"You have children though, right?"

"Yes, and I suppose that I have to get back to them."

"What do you think of the future for them?"

"Pretty good, so long as they can go to university. I recognize that I put that into jeopardy by coming here, but you have good lemon tea."

"And it is, in any case, too late for you, so you might as well enjoy your tea. It just would be nice if what was created here lasted, if there was some collective memory."

Léon, having finished his tea, gets up to leave: "That would ensure the legacy of the café, I imagine. Anyway, my parental obligations call me away."

* * *

Léon actually has very little to do to see his children off to school. His two daughters, Natalie and Eugenie, 15 and 17 years old respectively, have been perfectly capable of getting themselves up and going in the morning for quite some time. So, he just sits at the kitchen table and watches them. When Lora was there, the three would whirl around each other in a complex dance of coffee, toast and fruit. Now, it is hard to imagine that there was ever room for three, so fully his daughters seem to have blossomed to fill the space in the span of a day.

After two cursory "Bye dad"s, Natalie, always trailing her sister, slams the front door, leaving the house to settle into silence. Léon wonders how the absence of their mother will affect the girls in the longer term. Happy that today at least seems largely normal; he pulls out his notebook and scratches out a couple of ideas for an article or, more accurately, a feuilleton. Following Hervé's ideas, an open letter to the next generation of writers and artists tickles his fancy, something in a Rilkeen tone perhaps, losing himself in the pure irony that no one in that generation would ever see it, that the letter would just be a test to see if he could come up with some wisdom he might have imparted under different circumstances. He is not even sure that he would be capable of expressing such wisdom on paper.

Sitting in the same spot as he did countless times when he and Lora discussed family concerns, he is unable to write. As a couple, they decided a long time ago that he would protect their daughters as much as possible from the consequences of his actions and the subsequent state scrutiny. He did not leave his writing around the house, he did not bring up politics, he did not invite people who made the same sorts of choices to the house, etc. At the beginning, he chafed at the self-censorship. After a while, though, it became ordinary, automatic. It was almost comforting to know that the library had a wall of lockers for people like him, lockers that the police appreciated, since they contained a great deal of underground writing in a convenient, centralized location, but also resulted in a significant decrease in the number of searches at the house. Then there was an evening at the Unity for when the itch to talk politics just needed to be scratched. All in all, life was tolerable.

He had also been troubled by the thought that his daughters were being inculcated with some outdated ideal of purity belonging to a society where it would be scandalous for a proper young lady to read a novel. The reality was of course much more complex and far less sexist, but the undercurrent of promoting ignorance was not so different. As a result, he became more distant. He found that it was less frustrating to not pay much attention to what his girls were learning and it lessened the temptation to blurt out something inappropriate. This was why, even after the departure of Lora, expectations would be low for his involvement in their lives.

Things would be different if the girls could experiment freely without permanent consequences. That however is not how things work. Sure, they would likely not be followed and interrogated like he is, but everything questionable they did would be recorded and used against them at the Committee's convenience. If Eugenie was caught with an illegal book, there would likely only be a short interrogation and the confiscation of the book at the time. Ten years later though, if she had subversive tendencies that needed to be corrected by a stint in prison, the incident would be used at her trial. He and Lora decided some time ago that while they would support the girls if they chose to follow a path like his, they would not introduce things to them that might harm them or limit their options later on.

It doesn't quite make sense, as Hervé pointed out: how can someone reasonably decide to enter the Unity if they don't know the conifer table is in there? How would Eugenie know if she wants to read a book if she has never heard of it? Is knowing worth the price? Léon doesn't have any idea. It was for him, but Lora was never so sure. Following this path was not however fully her choice. It is important for both of them that, regardless of the lack of information, their daughters have some semblance of choice.

Léon has trouble disassociating the vague notion of young creative types from his daughters. Perhaps his distance from his children has allowed him to build up a nebulous fantasy about their future, a future that poetically transgresses the rules with impunity, a future that doesn't really take into account who they really are. In any case, his mind locks when he tries to break away from carefully respecting his family's rules. He stares at the basic ideas, then rips the page out of his notebook and sets it on fire.

Chapter 3

"Paetus, it does not hurt." Lora surreptitiously scratches the phrase on the immaculate table of the café she found across the street from the central park. Léon spoke occasionally about the tables at the Unity Café after the children had gone to bed, but she had never been inside. She had glimpsed them while walking by, but was careful not to show too much interest. It was best not to, what with the three black cars across the street. She had ordered a lemon tea to start, knowing full well that she disliked the taste. The aroma was what she imagined surrounded Léon as he transcribed all the ideas stored up from a day of forced silence on a blank page.

Stepping off the train at Kralovna, Lora entered a world where freight had the same priority as passengers. To her right, prefabricated cornices were being off-loaded; to her left, crates of what looked like some sort of medicine. The noise of all the machines, intensified by the echoing between the train and the station wall, was deafening. After a moment of disorientation, she spotted the door into the station and hurried in with her bags. Inside, the mechanical noise made way to the sounds of people walking, talking and laughing. "Doesn't everyone know that they can be overheard?" she silently mouthed, perplexed.

Suddenly, Claude was beside her. He grinned: "I've seen that reaction before. Besides the fact that this is not the capital, if you listen, you'll notice that almost everyone is talking about three things: the weather, farming and hockey. Anything else would be impractical.

"Anyway, I have to catch my next train. I just wanted to say that it was good to meet you. If you ever get out in the field we might run into each other again. Though I don't think the telephone should be our priority, it could be useful."

Then he was gone, lost in the crowd. Lora shrugged and made

her way to the street in front of the station. The apartment that was assigned would not be ready until that evening, so she resigned herself to getting to know the city. The station entrance opened to the center of the city, which was laid out in a grid. The street running along the front of the station seemed endless as she looked down it in both directions, blending into the fields at the edge of town. The wind was blowing along this infinite corridor, giving a slight sensation of movement as sounds passed. She shivered involuntarily, either from the coolness of the breeze or the vast open space, or both. Looking forward, her gaze was stopped by a wall of green in the distance. She decided to walk towards the wall, the enclosed space giving her a sense of comfort.

From the train station, she passed ornate government buildings of four to six stories that blended after a couple of blocks into two to three story low-key retail and offices. There was a steady stream of people on the sidewalk, but it was not busy. As in the station, people were animated and spoke to each other in a relatively loud voice, giving Lora the sensation that they took up more space than the crowds of the capital who spoke – when they conversed at all – in whispers and generally seemed as if they were trying to blend into the grey of the sidewalk. As she passed what looked like the central park, she noticed a café across the street. Her first reaction was to glance indirectly around, looking for the telltale three black cars. Not finding them, she found an empty bench in the park which gave her a good vantage point to study the café.

It took up both stories of a two story building, with big glass windows opening onto the street. Both stories looked half full. After a moment, she could no longer concentrate on the café, as the ever-present guilt that she might be doing something that would sully her record was becoming overwhelming. Barely an hour in this city and she was already willing to throw away everything for something she couldn't even pin down. Perhaps it was to feel closer to Léon, which was the exact opposite of what she needed to do. She needed to be the counterpoint to his insouciance. She needed to keep the family together and on the right path, even if that meant breaking it apart in the short term. Even if that meant leaving Natalie and Eugenie with a father so distant, who needed to hide so much from them.

Sitting in this park, she felt that she could trust everyone in her family but herself. Her daughters would probably not even feel her absence, so long as their daily habits remained the same. Everything would just continue as it always had. Léon would be alone at the kitchen table, but the conversations they repeated endlessly would echo in his ears. The other side of his life was already separated from the family; that would not change either, except in offering him another subject for his work. It was up to her to do the same, to continue her routine of ensuring that the family was kept on the normal side of the Committee ledgers, to maintain balance.

Lora sighed and pulled out the map where the location of her new apartment was noted. She would have to retrace her steps two blocks and then follow the cross-street east, one of the roads leading to the end of the world. She rose slowly, taking her time since the appointment was still an hour away, and as it provided an opportunity to scrutinize her surroundings a final time. It was not as if all cafés had the reputation of the Unity; there was simply no going back if it did and she went in. There were still no black cars, no one who had the air of an inspector. Ironically, she was by far the most suspicious-looking person there, which was another reason to not do anything potentially foolish.

The one bedroom apartment assigned by the Committee felt dead. It followed the standards, insofar as that was possible so far from the factories and given that it was in a converted house. Then there was the piano, a small upright Petrof that had seen better days, which did not as far as she knew follow the standards. Lora pulled out the bench and sat down, her back to the instrument. A collection of books sat in the shelves on the opposite wall, too varied to be the work of the Committee, even if it was undoubtedly combed through multiple times by inspectors. She took some photos of her family and the *Letters* out of her bag and placed them on a shelf at eye level. She wondered whether the piano was also brought in by former residents, perhaps the same people as those responsible for the books. The dull, functional furniture and uniform off-white paint covering the walls, including moldings, and the ceiling make the books and piano seem like poor attempts to add vitality to a moribund space.

The quiet stillness of the apartment gave Lora an atmosphere where she could focus on herself and realize that she was famished. After idly tapping the keys of the piano, she checked the kitchen for what else might have been left behind. Finding nothing, she looked up the nearest grocery store in the directory and left the house. The store was closed, as was every restaurant she passed. Spiraling outward, she found herself once more at the park, somber but for the halo of light emanating from the café. *Of course,* she thought, *though it is hard to imagine that everyone out at this time is abnormal.* She only hesitated for a moment, closing her eyes and taking a deep breath, before opening the door.

Lora stares at the phrase she just scratched into the surface of the table, savoring the scent of the lemon tea and letting her mind wander. When her stomach and curiosity become too insistent, she waves to the server. The server comes over with a smile on his face:

"You threw me for a moment with the tea, until it became obvious that you weren't actually drinking it."

Lora, taken aback by the forwardness, starts to ask what they have to eat when the server, still smiling, interrupts her.

"You'll want the goulash."

"I'm sorry?"

"We have sandwiches and goulash. Goulash is the comfort

food for people new in town."

"Fine. Bring me the goulash then." Lora turns away, hoping that the server takes the hint and stops talking.

Before going to the back to fill the order, the server says, "You can relax, you know. We are the only place open this late, everyone comes here."

Lora does not find the words reassuring. Sure, the space, simple and clean with light artistic touches, seems neutral and generally inviting. This is not how she would imagine what a den of poetic reprobates would look like. On the other hand, that means that the police could be here rather than sitting in their cars across the street. It was perhaps not a faux pas to enter the café, but she would have to do better at avoiding conversations like the one on the train.

"The goulash," the server announces, placing a plate of steaming stew and dumplings in front of Lora. "Enjoy."

He turns to leave, then hesitates and turns back: "All the normal folks from the capital have the same reaction to this place. We can tell when a train has come in by the strangers sitting on the benches in the park or passing on the sidewalk multiple times, trying to decide whether it is safe to come in. Normally, their stomachs decide for them, which is why the chef decided to add goulash to the late night menu. It usually takes a couple of weeks to acclimatize."

Lora, who has already hungrily dug into the food, nods distractedly. The nervous energy that had animated her throughout the day succumbs to the steadying weight of the meal. When the plate is empty, she leaves money on the table and heads out before the server has a chance to share more of his insight. Her work at the yard starts tomorrow, so sleep is the next priority on the list.

Chapter 4

The police were in the middle of searching the house when Natalie and Eugenie came home from school. Léon was sitting in the same place at the kitchen table as when they had left that morning, giving the impression that he was part of the furniture. He had in fact typed a dozen new copies of the current issue of the journal, sitting at the discrete fungus table at the Unity. With printing presses heavily regulated, each copy had to be typed individually, which was nothing if not painstaking. Those copies had already been passed on to a variety of interested parties, none of whom were of the next generation as far as Léon knew, though it was not exactly easy to track where the copies ended up. This was just as well, as it helped keep his ambitions modest.

The police had searched the house before, though the last time was several years ago. The girls were surprised, but did not act unduly perturbed as they came into the kitchen and joined their father at the table. The three of them sat silently, listening to the sounds of footsteps and furniture being opened and closed from other rooms, each lost in their own world.

After about half an hour, two inspectors join them at the table. One carries a small pile of books, which he places fastidiously on the table beside him, taking the time to line each up evenly with the spines facing the family. The other, looking slightly more authoritarian, waits for his partner to finish and then focuses his exaggeratedly narrowed eyes on each member of the family in turn. Natalie loses her composure and stares forlornly at the books, most of which are hers. Eugenie takes her sister's hand under the table.

Léon does not notice his daughters' discomfort and is nonplussed by the inspectors. "Had you mentioned you were coming, I would have bought some coffee. After so many cups the police have offered me, it would have been only fair."

The authoritarian inspector offers a friendly smile. "That is awfully nice of you to suggest it. Unfortunately, we can't arrange our visits in advance. Next time I will be sure to bring a vacuum flask."

"And next time, you can bring the book to be discussed. We can form a club."

"The Committee prefers that citizens are proactive in developing normal, healthy habits."

"What's wrong with my books?" Natalie blurts out.

He turns his smile to the teenager: "We all play important roles. My colleague and I, we collect materials that may be harmful to citizens. We also strongly encourage citizens to be vigilant so that our common environment can be free of unsafe materials. It is the responsibility of those at Central to determine the nature of the materials. Those that are deemed harmless will be returned."

Despite the pressure of Eugenie's hand, Natalie continues: "But why my books? Why not the books from all the other houses in the neighborhood?"

Léon intervenes before the authoritarian inspector can respond. "If you have run out of books to read at the library," he says, addressing the inspector, "we are of course very happy to provide you with others to peruse."

The inspector refocuses on Léon: "We of course do not read anything."

"Of course," Léon replies with a matching smile. "I expect that the books will be returned as soon as they are deemed inoffensive."

"Of course," the inspector says as he rises from the table. The other officer follows his lead, awkwardly collecting the meticulously piled books. "I am afraid that our business calls us elsewhere." He fixes Eugenie with his gaze as he continues, "Perhaps another house in the neighborhood."

The family sits in silence for a moment. Natalie pulls her hand out of Eugenie's grasp, holding back tears of anger. Eugenie stares at her father. Léon avoids eye contact. He feels as if he should say something, but nothing comes to mind. The visit was undoubtedly a warning, just in case he was tempted to bridge his two worlds and bring work or colleagues home now that Lora was absent. Yet it didn't make any sense. Dealing with the searches and confiscations was part of his work, so it was really the police that were bringing it into the house. And failing to find evidence of his guilt, without his manuscripts to confiscate, they felt it necessary to take Natalie's books, all approved by the Committee, just so they didn't have to leave empty handed. The least they could have done was to bring something from his locker at the library to plant, though that might have been difficult seeing as he was sure that they had already catalogued everything in the locker. In any case, the logic is straightforward, if one accepts certain premises, but it is not exactly as if the basics of how the state actually functions is taught in school.

Léon finally shrugs and jokes, "Well, at this rate, we should be inspector-free for another five years or so."

It is Eugenie's turn to be angry: "This is going to be in the paper tomorrow, everyone at school is going to know. What did you do?"

"Nothing." What else could he say?

"They don't search houses for nothing. What did you do?"

"Nothing. And you didn't do anything, and there is nothing wrong with Natalie's books. The police are people too, just as prone to error as the rest of us."

"I'm going to be shunned because of a mistake? That's not possible."

"I don't know how else to explain it. Anyway, it might be hard at school for a while, but the kids will move on to other things soon enough. Just make sure that you don't actually do something that will end up in your file. That is what would haunt you."

"How am I going survive tomorrow?" Eugenie asks plaintively, imagining being singled out by teachers and treated like a leper by her friends.

Léon resists the temptation to ask how Eugenie has treated other kids whose families appeared in the police column of the official newspaper. He hopes that the experience makes her more understanding, though it is just as likely that she will become cruel, overcompensating to keep her place in the microcosm. He would put a wager on which direction she would go, just between him and himself, only he wasn't exactly privy to her school life. It would probably make for an interesting story, so it is for the best that he doesn't know so as to avoid the frustration of not being able to tell it.

Léon begins to feel an urge to go to the library to see if the police did actually visit his locker, an urge no doubt partially motivated by his discomfort in seeing his daughters so distraught and having absolutely no idea what to say or do. Lora was so much better at this sort of thing. Of course, she was also better at avoiding these sorts of situations. After a moment of indecision, he rises and starts to leave.

"Where are you going?" Eugenie asks suspiciously.

Léon hesitates, then decides that there is no harm in telling the truth: "The library."

Natalie chimes in, suddenly serious: "I am going with you. They took my books."

"All right." Books were after all the principal reason for the place. He would just have to find a moment alone to check the locker.

Natalie turns to her sister: "You should come too, Eugenie."

Eugenie looks around. The officers were careful, leaving everything as far as possible where they found it. For Eugenie, that actually made things worse than had they made a mess. In cleaning up, she could have in a sense remade the house her own. With everything still in place, the home as she has known it is thrown open to strangers, the spots where she could retreat from everyone suddenly felt on display. And everyone would know tomorrow. She nods dispiritedly at her sister and goes to find her coat.

The library is a dozen blocks away, the first three stories of a squat tower meant to symbolize modern progress. Its unadorned, reinforced concrete exterior is a great example of a modernism bereft of imagination. Whether this can be construed as progress is a discussion that comes up regularly at the Unity. The eternal disagreement on the subject boils down to whether progress can be a movement towards anything or if it must head in a particular direction, whether society is meandering, driven by a grab bag of short and medium-term goals, or if it is, as the Committee suggests, marching directly towards the end of history. It is nice to believe that one's writing is part of some grand movement to a better world, though it is difficult to reconcile the belief with the reality that the more one produces and the more broadly one's writings are distributed, the closer one is to being locked up. Léon continues to be surprised that he and the others incapable of this conviction still find the motivation to write.

Natalie, unable to stand the morose silence of her sister and the distracted silence of her father, starts to recount the story of the novel she was in the middle of reading before it was confiscated.

"There's this guy who is really clever and rich. He started out as a cooper. I had to look that up. Is a cooper even a thing, these days? Yeah, the story took place about a hundred years ago, I guess. Anyway, he acquires farmland, vineyards, woods, all sorts of stuff that he can make more money from. He also lends money on the side. All sorts of things. He is part of a group of local vineyard owners who are supposed to negotiate together but when he learns that some traders are really desperate to buy, he goes ahead and negotiates a great price alone, at the expense of everyone else. Nobody stays mad at him though, because he hides his money and lives simply.

"And he hides all this from his family. His wife and daughter don't even realize the extent of what's going on. They are essentially living in poverty and just sort of accept it. They don't know any better, they don't go out, they're useless except in spreading the lie of their lack of money. They're supposed to be spiritual or something, like nuns. Then a cousin comes to visit and the daughter falls in love. I guess it was okay to marry first cousins back then. That was probably why they were spiritual. So, she falls in love, which motivates her to do other things, defy her father mostly. It's all in stupid little ways, but whatever. If a girl spends her days crocheting and going to church and never steals food from the pantry or fruit from the orchard, what can I expect?"

"It was a long time ago," Eugenie says.

"Yeah, I get that," Natalie replies, "I'm sure glad we didn't live back then. And maybe by the end of the book, she will have grown up to be less frustrating and weak. If I ever finish the book."

After a moment of silence, she continues: "I didn't get the father though. If he had become so greedy that everyone and everything was only valuable for the money he could get out of them, why didn't he treat his daughter the same way? Why did he just treat her as another mouth to feed rather than as an investment? With some education, her chances for a good marriage could have been so much better. She could have also kept the second house he had acquired or, I don't know, hosted gatherings to improve relations with the neighbors he had slighted. Maybe I just don't get how people thought back then."

"We've arrived," Léon announces, opening the door for the girls to enter. "Why don't you girls go get what you want and we can meet back here."

"Okay," Natalie replies, dragging her sister up the stairs to the anemic literature section.

Léon starts walking towards the lockers, then changes direction to flip through the current periodicals. He can't bring himself to even approach his locker with his daughters so close. He looks for newspapers from Kralovna. Finding three, he takes them and sits at a table. Predictably, all three have the same content, even if their layout and pictures are quite different. Beyond a brief list of local events, all the articles seemed to be imported from the capital. No local culture, society or opinions. A dry recounting of a collision, the construction of a new building, etc. do nothing to make him feel closer to Lora. It is in fact the opposite; the lack of information on how people there live increases immeasurably the distance he feels between them.

The sound of a pile of books dropped on the table wakes him from his reverie. The girls are standing across from him, bemused. After flashing a sheepish smile, his brow furrows as he recognizes the books.

"Those books look awfully familiar," he observes.

"We couldn't find two of them," Natalie says.

Léon scratches his chin.

"I am not going to stop reading just because the police came and took my books away."

"Haven't you already read most of them?"

"I am not going to live without these books just because the police came and took them away."

"It's not as if it matters now," Eugenie adds. "And a library wouldn't have anything that was not allowed anyway."

"If that's true, the inspectors must have been mistaken when they took the books," Léon suggests.

"I guess," Eugenie replies reluctantly, "but it's not as if it was their job to know what they were taking. They aren't familiar with every book in existence."

"Perhaps then they should wait until whatever they confiscate is judged before putting anything in the police column."

"Yeah," she barely whispers, dejected. She turns to Natalie:

"Let's get out of here."

Natalie checks out her books and the three head home. Despite the fading light, Natalie's nose is already in the book she had described earlier. Eugenie would occasionally give her sister a course correction so she didn't run into anything. Despite the inevitability of being shunned the next day, the replacement of the books gives both sisters the sense that they still have some control over the situation.

Léon is relieved that neither of his daughters noticed that he really didn't do anything at the library. He could have lied had the question come up, saying that he was looking for some news from Kralovna, but that might have led to awkward questions regarding Lora's situation that he would have had difficulty answering. He wishes that she was his Arria, that her courage and sacrifice had led her to be obstinately at his side. She is only his Arria insofar as she offers him an example of how to live courageously. Their situations are so different though, that he is not sure what courage is in his case. It seems almost meaningless without beliefs and ideals.

When they get home, Léon cooks up some rice, mixes in some vegetables and a bit of sausage, and they take their usual places at the table. Natalie still has her nose in the book and eats distractedly, rarely bringing the spoon all the way to her mouth. Eugenie picks at her food before giving up. Normally she would ask her mother for permission to leave the table, so, for form, she asks her father. Léon, eating with his usual generous appetite, replies "of course" with a quick smile and then immediately refocuses on his plate. Natalie follows her sister without bothering to ask, leaving Léon to clean up. Once they are gone, he pulls out his notebook and jots down some ideas for his contribution to the next issue of the journal.

Chapter 5

Lora listens to a heated discussion coming clearly through the wall between the local head of logistics and the supplier out from the capital for the day. She is sitting on a bench in the hallway of the administration building for the Department of Telephones' yard, waiting for the person who is supposed to show her around. At first she tries to ignore the argument – she doesn't want to be anywhere near conflict, as that could jeopardize her position – but the thin wall and raised voices makes it impossible.

"Just use the bloody galvanized iron wire."

"What a stupid suggestion. You know that the iron doesn't work over these distances. You promised us copper months ago. Where the hell is it?"

"And you know that we have to import copper and crossbars. Your precious system is not more important than border security."

"My precious system? It is a Committee priority, for fuck's sake."

"Everything is a Committee priority. Even living in this godforsaken hole, you should know that."

"This literally helps put food on the table. How is that not more important than other projects?"

"You're delusional. We have enough grain now for the country's needs. Assuming that the telephone improves on that – which is questionable at best – it will all be for export. That would be nice, but to consider it a priority is just stupid. Do you want the iron or not?"

"Is it twisted pair?"

"Of course."

"So long as it doesn't cost me anything and it doesn't bump us down the list for copper."

The supplier lowers his voice to a more normal level: "That

brings us to crossbars…"

At that moment a side door opens and a man and woman enter the building. As they walk towards Lora, the man narrows his eyes. When they are standing in front of her, he says with a tinge of anger, "If I didn't know any better, I'd say that you are the judge who sent me to prison."

Lora's face reddens and her heart sinks. *So much for avoiding conflict*, she thinks. To the man, she replies, "It must have been a long time ago, I don't recall."

"His name is Maurice Butterfield, if that helps," the woman says. "And I'm Anna, never been to jail myself. You must be Lora; welcome to our little world."

"I don't recall," Lora repeats.

"Yeah, well, whatever, follow us. We have to load poles today."

They go out into the yard. It is mostly uncovered and filled with wooden poles. One end is defined by a spur railway line, where two empty flat cars sits. The other end is filled with crossbars and spools of wire. Elevated rails for suspended cranes crisscross the space. Across from the administration building, a sheltered area contains a variety of exchanges and other equipment. The trio head to the closest pile of poles to the train car.

"These," Anna explains, "are our standard poles: cedar, forty feet long, about eleven hundred pounds. The car can hold thirty of them." She then drags a crane over and demonstrates how to attach the pole, hoist it up, drag it over to the car, and place it cleanly. "It is pretty simple. Just let the crane do all the work. If a pole slips, just get out of the way. Don't try to stop it. Questions?"

Lora shakes her head.

"Okay. We will do this together, you take that end." She points to the far end of the log. "Maurice, do you want to start with the next pile for the other car?"

"Sure, happy to leave you with the judge."

As Maurice wanders over to another crane and pulls it to an adjacent pile, Anna makes sure that Lora has attached her end of the log to the crane properly. Once the two ends are secure, she hoists up the pole and the two pull it to the car together. They work at a slow, measured pace, partially because nothing about moving poles, especially with a new person, lends itself to speed, partially because nothing ever happens quickly in the yard. If they loaded the cars too quickly, they would have to wait around until the railway workers came to take these away and bring new ones.

The work is done mostly in silence, since the three are too far from each other to speak normally. Lora is relieved; Anna seems fine, but she dreads any more interactions with Maurice. She tries distracting herself by thinking of what she would write to the family that evening, but very little comes to mind. She can't write anything of consequence, since there is a good chance that it would be read by third parties. Everything of inconsequence has been colored either by sensitive subjects, from the conversation about how the railways were run on the train to Kralovna to the copper wire argument, or by her paranoia, spending hours on a bench across from the café or in even thinking about writing a letter, so nothing seems safe. Slowly, she loses herself in the rhythm of the work and the discomfort she is already feeling, doing serious manual labor for the first time in her life.

At more or less noon, Anna calls for lunch and the three head back through the administrative building, then across the street into a building that looks like a bunker. Once inside, they enter a cozy, bustling cafeteria. The energy reminds Lora of the train station, showing that this is really how open people are around here. *This will take some time to get used to*, she thinks.

As they join the line, Anna explains, "This is the exchange building. All the telephone lines from the region go to the exchange in the basement, from which there is a direct line to the capital. You probably noticed that the building looks like a bunker, that's because we get tornadoes once in a while. The last one destroyed the exchange, which made it difficult to coordinate aid. That was when the system only had a couple of thousand poles. We just passed 45,000 poles this year, and that's not counting the ones farmers put up, so if we lost the exchange now, it would be terrible."

"There isn't any back-up?"

"Yeah, but none of the other machines have all the features. This one was imported so that the local engineers would have something to copy. Originally, it wasn't even supposed to be hooked up, but the engineers wanted to study how it functioned in the real world. Since then, nobody has seriously suggested replacing it. I suspect that the department conveniently loses the directive the Committee probably gives them to do so. The directive is all for form though, the reality doesn't matter for a machine in the basement of a building seven hundred kilometers from the capital."

Lora accepts Anna's opinion regarding the Committee with more aplomb than she was able to with Claude on the train. "You seem to be quite knowledgeable about how things work around here. How long have you been working in the yard?"

"A couple of years, I guess, but you won't learn much here. I got almost all I know from helping bring our local lines up to standard when I was on the farm. They just chopped down a bunch of trees, stuck them in the ground along the road and then strung spare barbed wire between them. A basic party line, where everybody could hear everybody else, but it worked okay. Helped spread the word about which elevator operators were the least corrupt that year. The department wouldn't let us connect to the network with that setup though, so we couldn't even phone into town if there was an emergency. When the group had enough money to improve our loop, I volunteered to go through the manual and figure out what we needed to do."

"I don't understand. So, the government doesn't set up the telephone system?"

"Sure, in and between the towns. Beyond that the farmers have to do things themselves." Anna shrugs. "You know, it's always been that way. We built the roads, put together the funds for the local medical clinic; the government doesn't have the money to do all that and in any case doesn't have a clue as to what we need. Why should telephones be any different?"

They reach the counter and take the plates that the cooks pass to them, then find an open table.

"Why did you leave the farm?"

"With the new harvesters and the like, farming doesn't need a lot of people anymore. Besides, we realized that it is better to have some of our own in the system that the government understands. Most of those who left joined the crews to stay in the countryside, but I don't like traveling around all the time."

"The crews?"

"The workers who build the government roads, utilities, and all the rest between the towns."

"Ah."

Anna and Lora haven't yet touched their food, while Maurice wipes up the last bit of sauce with a slice of bread.

"Maurice," Anna says, "aren't you quiet today. Since you are finished, why don't you entertain us while we eat?"

Maurice looks at her and shakes his head.

"I've never seen you so shy in mixed company," Anna teases.

Lora sees her sentiments in Maurice's expression; an ingrained distrust towards everyone and an aversion towards expressing himself. However, while Lora has resigned herself to them, Maurice seems frustrated. She tries to intervene: "Let's leave Maurice alone."

Instead of calming him, the words are taken as a provocation. Maurice says quietly but forcefully, "I'd say that you ruined my life, but we both know that's a lie. Judges are puppets and everyone is guilty of something; I knew I was going to prison the minute I was arrested. But it doesn't change anything; you were the one handed down the judgment."

He then takes his dishes and leaves the table.

Anna is stunned for a moment, but quickly decides that it would be best to just finish the meal. She has never witnessed this sort of conflict, chalking up the nature of the people from the capital to the cold isolation of a big city. She didn't know that Maurice had been in prison until that morning and everything about it was making her uncomfortable yet curious. She had at first dismissed it, but after Maurice's outburst she feels both the need to know what happened and a certain fear as to what it could have been.

Lora also focuses on finishing her food. Then she focuses on surviving the day, with the increasing inability of her body to respond to her mind's commands. The trio manage nonetheless to finish stacking the logs on the cars. Lora just watches as Anna and Maurice strap them down. With that done, Maurice heads into the administration building to complete the paperwork and Anna approaches her.

"Besides the awkwardness, that was a good day. It's not complicated, but some people take a while to catch on." She pauses and then whispers, "Why was Maurice in jail?"

"That's for him to tell you." Even had Lora wanted to tell Anna, she wouldn't have been able to as she had forgotten everything concerning Maurice's trial long ago.

"Right," Anna says, disappointed, before continuing with enthusiasm, "You must be really tired. I'll see you tomorrow!"

She disappears through a small door in the external wall, leaving Lora alone among the poles. She closes her eyes and breathes deeply, trying to find the energy to walk home. *Tomorrow should be better*, she thinks as she forces one foot in front of the other, *and next week, and next month*.

Arriving home, she makes it as far as the piano and lies on the hard wooden bench. Her body is uniformly in pain, so she isn't able to feel the difference between the bench and a soft mattress. The futility of what she is doing, trying to keep in the good graces with the Committee, to be without fault, blends with the physical pain and she starts crying softly. The sounds echo off the bare, foreign walls, reminding her of how alone she is, how the space here goes on forever.

The light is fading outside when she sits up and contemplates the photos of her family on the shelves on the other side of the room. She searches in one of her bags for a pen and paper. Finding them, she sits at the kitchen table and begins to write the letter she contemplated earlier in the day:

Dear Léon,

I am inclined to believe that our friend Pliny was right. Yes, Arria stabbing herself in the gut did take a great deal of courage, but even with her long held resolve to die a glorious death it was the courage of a moment, it did not have to persist and weather the efforts – as much self-inflicted as external – to break her resolve. I would also like to think that there would be two Arrias if a modern version of the story was to be written, etc.

Chapter 6

Léon sits on the stairs listening to Eugenie crying softly in her room, the letter from Lora in his hand. This is the third night in a row that Léon has sat here, listening to his daughter, feeling powerless to do anything. Being close to her, comforting her, would only make the barrier between his two worlds thinner and make the possibility that she would have to endure more experiences like this increasingly likely. Even after so many years of distance, he finds that it is a struggle to not rush in and take her into his arms, to make sure that she knows that she is not alone, that he is there for her.

The letter strengthens the feeling of powerlessness. Léon appreciates Lora's support in considering both of them Arria and suggesting that the greatest courage is in continual, long term efforts. He does not feel in any way courageous, conflicted would be a better word. The more important issue though is that she feels the need – rightly of course – to write to him with the gloss of discussing Pliny. Pliny means nothing to him, there are no details that give him a sense of what she is really going through. He knows that she is having a difficult time, that much is clear, but nothing more. It is as frustrating as trying to find details about Kralovna at the library. There isn't enough content to empathize, let alone sympathize, with what she is going through. Even if there was, he would not risk, any more than she would, putting it in a letter. So he sits on the stairs in the middle of the night with the nebulous knowledge that she could use some support beyond some vague allusions hidden in a discussion about an ancient Roman text.

Léon starts to wonder if he couldn't create his own Plinian letter whole cloth that could come closer to expressing something meaningful to his wife when the door to Natalie's room opens. He sees her for an instant haloed in the weak light of her bedside lamp before she heads downstairs. She stops with a start a step from him; his presence finally penetrated the gloom and her sleep-dulled mind.

"Dad, are you awake?" she asks in a whisper.

"Yeah," he whispers back.

"Why didn't you say anything? I could have tripped over you."

"Sorry, my thoughts were elsewhere."

"Your thoughts are always elsewhere," she replies as she makes her way around him and into the kitchen. When she reaches the doorway, she turns to ask, "Have you heard from mom?"

"Yeah," he repeats, holding out the letter.

After turning on the kitchen light, she takes the letter and then sits down at the table to read it. Once she is done, she turns to her father and says, "I don't understand."

"It is from an ongoing discussion your mother and I were having about courage. She is very strong, sacrificing her time with you and Eugenie to be where she is needed the most to help the country."

"Yeah, I get that. You guys repeated it enough times before she left. The stabbing thing is new though, and kind of disturbing. But why wouldn't she just say that she got there okay and, I don't know, that she loved us?"

"Well, she read Pliny's book on the train, I gave it to her the night before she left, so she probably wanted to say something about it before she forgot. Once she's settled in, I'm sure that she will write to both you and your sister. Though, to be honest, I would have thought that you would have appreciated the historical obscurity."

Natalie shrugs, goes to the sink to drink a glass of water, then heads back upstairs. She murmurs a barely audible "night, dad" before disappearing. Léon turns off the light and heads to his room a moment later, relieved to not hear crying as he passes

Eugenie's door.

The next day both girls appear tired, but they still don't miss a beat in their morning ritual. Léon, in a similar state, still manages to have a productive day, writing new material at the obscure fungus table of the Unity. Hervé has not mouthed a word about his ambitions to indoctrinate the youth and immortalize his establishment and Léon has found himself less and less preoccupied by his new role as single parent. Excepting the idea germinating in the back of his mind to write letters in the style of Pliny, he has returned to his usual themes of daily life as a blacklisted writer, themes on which he has been able to scribble effortlessly over the years.

At the end of the day, Léon heads to the library to drop off his feuilletons. He pauses to go through the papers in his locker for the first time since the police visited the house. He is absorbed by a forgotten piece that might be pretty good with a bit of editing when he hears "Dad?" from behind him. He turns to see Natalie standing there, a bit perplexed, with a copy of *The Letters of Pliny the Younger* in her hand. Léon smiles at her while blindly putting what he was reading in the locker and closing the door.

"Why do you have a locker here? Why were you in such a hurry to close it?" Natalie asks in the low voice typical to public spaces in the capital.

"Oh, just for some scribblings, it's more convenient to keep them here than at home, and some of them are embarrassingly bad."

"Is this what the police were looking for?"

"That would be strange. I guess we'll know if I show up here one day and they are gone. No, that doesn't work since they took your books, which were clearly not what they were after. Maybe I should take my papers to Central myself to see what they think. I might have a dirty limerick or two in there that they might not take kindly to." Léon continues the train of ideas in his head, concluding that this might actually make for an amusing story for a future journal issue. He resists pulling out his notebook to jot it down.

"I still think it is strange that you have a locker here."

"Yeah, you're probably right. Why don't you check the book out? You can come with me to the grocery store if you'd like. I have to pick up some things for dinner."

"Okay," Natalie says as they walk towards the front.

When they are in the street, Léon notices the tell-tale three black cars parked across the street. His heart sinks and his mind scrambles to find some sort of explanation for them if they start following him.

"What do you write?" Natalie asks, oblivious to the police presence. "I'm sure that it isn't dirty limericks."

"I don't really write anything, not being a member of the guild," Léon replies more for the benefit of anyone who might be listening than for his daughter. "Have you started Pliny?"

"Yes, just the first couple of letters."

"What do you think of it?"

"It is sometimes hard to follow; the customs are strange, but also oddly familiar. It isn't what I expected, from reading mom's letter."

"No, I suppose not. And with the book you were describing the other day, did the daughter have more strength of character by the end?"

Natalie is taken aback by the fact that her father remembered what she had said. "Sort of: her parents died and she did become the head of the household. She did put her mark on her town, spending her money on schools, improvements to the church, that sort of thing. She was sort of betrayed by her first love, though really, her expectations were ridiculous, had a short, loveless marriage until her husband died, and then kind of fell back into the nun thing. Maybe she was always that way; it's not as if she consummated her marriage or anything. It was like a living death; just existing, feeling miserable, being a good

Christian, waiting to die to be released from her life, maybe even be happy. So, not really I guess.

"It would have been more frustrating had I cared about the character at the end, but she barely had a personality. There were some glimpses of cleverness, but they were motivated once again by her idiotic incestuous puppy love."

"So you are happy to be done with it then?"

"Not really. It's fun to snipe. And with fictional characters, nobody's feelings get hurt."

"Ah." The reflection in the windows of the grocery store as they approach shows that the cars were not at the library specifically for him. He hides his relief in his typical smile.

Natalie smiles back, feeling both a rare connection to her father and a renewed sense that she really doesn't know him at all. "I'm just going to stay out here and read."

"Okay." Léon replies distractedly, already putting the conversation behind him and focusing on what to buy.

When Léon and Natalie arrive home, Eugenie is sitting at the kitchen table waiting for them. In a serious voice, she asks them to sit. They obey after putting the groceries on the counter.

"What do you do all day, dad?" Eugenie asks when they are settled. "Someone asked me today, and I didn't know what to answer. I never know what to answer, but I guess it didn't used to matter. But now, with mom gone, I think that we should know."

"Fair point, but you will be disappointed. I don't do much of anything, I don't have a job. You might recall from when you were much younger that I used to write, but those days are long gone. I lost my muse. Happily..."

"Is that why you don't want anyone to look in your locker?" Natalie interjects, joining the interrogation. "Are you ashamed of what you write now?"

"What locker?" Eugenie asks her sister, caught by surprise.

"Oh, he has a locker filled with writing at the library."

"Look," Leon says, trying to take control of the conversation, "I do not write any more. I spend my days in cafés drinking lemon tea, observing the tableau of modern life that passes by. Once in a while, I scribble a note or two that I have taken to leaving in a locker at the library so they do not clutter the house. It is important to repeat that that is not writing; I am not, and have not been for quite some time, a writer."

Léon pauses before continuing: "Happily, I did earn enough money back then to contribute to making sure that you have a roof over your heads. This is of course in addition to getting the groceries and cooking. Speaking of which, can I put the groceries away and start making dinner?"

"Hold on," Eugenie orders, regaining her composure. She pulls a copy of an issue of the journal dating back seven months.

"Interesting," Léon says, immediately intrigued by the possibility of at least partially resolving the enigma of where the journal goes when it leaves the Unity circle. It also could shed some light on how someone who does not know that a publication exists comes to acquire and, presumably, read it. "Who gave you that?"

"You lied to us," Eugenie responds angrily. "What does it matter how I got it?"

Léon's train of thought goes further: now that they know about his writing, he doesn't have to keep his two worlds separate. Life for him may be much easier from now on, but he isn't convinced. If the authorities did not yet know she had the journal, her record could still be kept clean. If it was already too late, he would have to try to control how they do things in the future to minimize negative repercussions. It wouldn't be a great idea to leave illegal reading materials around the house, for instance.

Then Léon's thoughts reach Lora and he has a moment of panic. Everything she has been doing has been to ensure that the family has stayed sufficiently in the Committee's good graces so the girls' futures would not be compromised, so that they could go to university and have as many options open to them as possible throughout their lives. They had talked about one of the girls coming across an illegal book and being interested in it, and they knew that they would support her if she decided to continue along that line. They didn't think of the possibility that the interest would come simply from her father's involvement in it, rather than from the content or the lifestyle or the anti-government sentiment or a million other things. His thoughts circle around to the only hope being that the interest is fleeting and that nobody of consequence knows about it.

Léon brings his mind back to the conversation: "Well, of course I lied to you. You could go to prison just for having it. If the police showed up now, we would all be in a difficult situation. Eugenie, who knows you have this?"

"Don't try to focus on me. You have been involved in writing this journal for years. You are the reason the police watch us. It is your fault that the police searched the house and my life is over." Eugenie underlines the anger in her words by ripping the journal from the hands of Natalie, who had quietly slid it across the table and had started thumbing through it.

Léon takes the journal from Eugenie in turn. For dramatic effect, he goes to the stove and lights an element, which he uses to set it on fire. He opens the window and then waits until the journal is adequately consumed by the flames before dropping it into the sink and turning on the faucet. He feels sad about the loss of a copy, but vaguely remembers that that issue did not contain feuilletons he would ever consider brilliant.

Leaning against the counter, he turns to his daughters and attempts to imitate Lora: "Anything that I have done and continue to do is my business, and no trace of it is welcome in this house or in your possession. My record was compromised a long time ago, when I was a writer and the Committee decided that what I wrote was not becoming of a citizen of this country.

Your records, as well as your mother's, are clean. So long as they stay that way, your lives are full of possibilities. Eugenie, your difficulties at school are not going to last. Natalie, the police are going bring back your books. And now I am going to put away the groceries and make dinner."

Léon decides that pressing Eugenie to tell him who gave her the journal would not lead to anything but more conflict, so he lets it drop. A moment later, he is surprised to see her joining him at the counter to put the food away. He glances back at the table, where Natalie's nose is back in Pliny's *Letters*. He is at a loss to explain their reaction to what he said, words that seem to him hollow and hypocritical. He has every intention to continue to distribute the journal, fully aware that that puts his family's future in doubt.

Chapter 7

Lora drags herself out of the house for another dinner at the café she went to on her first day in town. After so many years of Léon getting groceries and preparing meals, she finds it easier to go out to eat. The café turns out to be open every time her stomach becomes insistent, so she does not expend the little energy she has at the end of the day to find other places. She figures that once she gets used to the physical nature of her new job, she will be more motivated to find food elsewhere. She recognizes that she was just as exhausted in the capital, even if it was moral fatigue rather than physical effort that left her drained. She still holds out hope that life here will be less mentally wearing, despite the distance from her family and the situation with Maurice.

As she enters the café, she remembers Léon explaining how he would pause and reflect on which table would best suit his mood and intentions before choosing where to sit. When the room isn't busy, she just makes a beeline for the table on which she had scratched Arria's famous quote. While she has been making some progress in adapting to the more open culture of the city, it is limited to not being shocked by people's conversations and how loud they speak, as well as to asking Anna endless questions. Her mood has not fundamentally changed since her arrival, making sitting at the same table appropriate, even though she doesn't actually follow Léon's system.

Today though the café is packed with people; it is the first time that the grumbling of her stomach has coincided with typical dinner hours. The ambiance seems strange in a way that takes her a moment to pinpoint. Everyone is either not speaking or conversing in hushed tones. It is a microcosm of capital induced paranoia in the midst of an open field, as comforting as the goulash for transplants like her. It is also disconcerting, since it acts as a reminder of the uphill battle she faces leaving that part of her behind.

A server passes and points to a table with an open seat. She recognizes Maurice, deep in conversation with a woman she has never seen before. Driven by hunger, the lack of choice and the fact that she manages to eat lunch with him every day, she approaches the table and asks if she can sit. Maurice responds with a curt nod, and does not introduce his companion. It is actually more comfortable to have a meal with him here since Anna is not around; they can indulge in their taciturn side without being needled by someone endlessly curious to know more about her past as a judge and his time in prison.

Lora introduces herself to the woman and learns all that is polite to know about her. Her name is Violet, is in Kralovna for a week on Committee business – a trip she takes every month or two – and enjoys what she refers to as the entrepreneurial socialism that gives the region its energy. Everything about her countenance gives the sense that she has followed the official path without deviation, yet her evident link to Maurice hints at something more. There is generally some leeway when one works with or is married to someone with a questionable record, but little when one voluntarily sees that someone as a friend. It is undoubtedly not quite the same so far from the capital, but still seems an unnecessary risk for a person with an unblemished record.

In an effort to keep Violet talking, Lora brings up the hopefully neutral subject of having a piano in her apartment: "It was a bit strange; I guess that I expected a standard apartment with perhaps some minor embellishments from the previous tenants. A piano is something else though, makes me wish I could play. Have you run into anything like that?"

Maurice manages to become more somber and suspicious in reaction to her words. Violet, in contrast, responds favorably. "In my experience, it has mainly been large plants that people have left behind. I was in one place where there was a plant in an enormous pot with long, waxy leaves tucked away in a corner on the floor. It looked like a mop, the leaves drooped so much. I dragged it over to a window and gave it some water, and in a couple of weeks most of the leaves were pointing almost straight up. It ended up being about five feet tall, still disheveled though; it definitely gave the place some character."

The conversation continues with the description of other unique finds, confirming that Violet moves around a great deal, but not much else. As Lora has lived a far more sedentary life, she has far less to contribute and more time to eat. In the end, despite arriving after Maurice and Violet, she finishes and, after politely excusing herself, is the first to leave the table. She glances over at the table where she had scratched Arria's phrase, looking alien with a small group of men leaning in to discuss something quietly though – if their gestures are any indication – passionately. She is relieved when she finds herself in the street, which feels strange since her initial reaction to the microcosm was comfort. She reflects on the possibility that she is changing more than she first thought. Regardless, now that her stomach is sated, her desire for sleep pulls her back to her apartment.

* * *

"Lora," Anna calls out as Lora enters the yard the next morning, "the head of logistics would like to see you. It is the third door on the right in the admin building."

Lora heads back into the building and knocks on the door of the office. She has learned a lot since the first day, sitting on the bench listening to the discussion on wire; including the relative conductivity of iron, versus steel or copper – copper has at least four times better conductivity than the other metals – and how twisting individual wires together prevents cross-talk; but most aspects of the telephone system are still a mystery to her. In this context, she does not know how to take the head of logistics' request.

The office looks more like a war room, with a central table littered with papers and maps showing present and future lines of all kinds; telephone, telegraph, railway, road, etc.; as well as depots, warehouses, areas within rights-of-way large enough to dump poles and other equipment. There are also running inventories and order lists – both orders the Department has made to suppliers and those received by the Department by crews and farmer syndicates. Lora feels immediately overwhelmed, barely registering the meticulous looking man at the center of the whirlwind of information. He notices her distraction and gives her a moment to look around before asking if she would like to sit down and offering his name: Phillip Shirreff.

"The reason that I asked for you to come see me," he begins, coming straight to the point, "is that I am going to a meeting with the railroads this morning and I think you should come along. Given your background, you might have some useful insights."

"My background?"

"In the midst of capital politics. According to your file, you did very well. Which is of course to say that there is very little in the file."

"Is this what the Committee wants my role to be?"

"The Committee takes a hands-off approach to our work, since they have limited knowledge of how things function around here and little desire to expend the resources to change that. I suspect, since they have a habit of sending us nuisance cases, that it's a bit more complicated, but that's neither here nor there. The point being that the Committee does not have a specific plan for you."

So long as I keep my head down, Lora thinks. To Phillip: "What would you expect me to do?"

"Be a fly on the wall. You evidently aren't yet very familiar with the telephone system, so there is no point in getting involved in the discussion. After, you can let me know if there were subtleties that I may have missed. There might be nothing of course, I just have a hunch that there is more going on. In return, you can avoid working in the yard for half a day. And, at worst, the only thing that can be added to your file is a note saying that you attended."

Lora is enticed by the idea. As a judge, she was a public face of the justice system, while others in the shadows actually pulled the strings. Here was an opportunity to reverse the role; she might actually be able to have a real influence on decisions. The central motivation of coming out was to keep her record cleaner than clean in order to ensure an open future for her daughters. The reassignment was at the limit of her power at the time, power that broke up her family geographically but was hopefully going to keep it together in other ways. She knew that while she had been able to keep herself in the clear in the capital, it was only a matter of time before that was compromised. Maurice was of course correct in saying that everyone was guilty – she knew that better than most. She had presided over more than one trial of a fellow judge. In any case, she feels that she is getting ahead of herself. She can't see a significant downside to attending the meeting, so she decides to accept Phillip's offer and see where it goes.

"Okay," Lora replies, "on one condition: you say nothing about the Committee that could be interpreted as a criticism or as a suggestion that they do not have full control over the region."

"But I can criticize the railroads?"

"Low level policy and operations, yes; strategic direction, no."

"I can work with that. Let's go."

The meeting is to be held in the small office complex above the train station. Phillip and Lora arrive ten minutes late, entering a room filled with managers of each rail line running in part or wholly in the region. The Committee had set up the system so that, while all the lines were under the same state banner, only the main lines, essentially lines connecting to the capital or between regions, were controlled centrally at a high level in the bureaucratic hierarchy. The secondary lines, those that neither crossed regional boundaries nor connected to the capital, had dispersed, lower level management. They both sit at the table and pass another ten minutes with introductions.

Then the door opens and Violet enters. As she discreetly makes her way to a chair along the wall, her eyes betray an instant of surprise to find Lora at the table. The railroad people on the other hand do not seem at all surprised by Violet's attendance. Lora views the presence of the mystery woman as the fifth piece of a thousand piece puzzle; close enough to the beginning that it only makes sense to note it, saving trying to make sense of everything for much later.

Phillip controls the agenda, moving as efficiently as possible, given the number of people present, through the four main areas of overlap between railroads and telephones: freight costs and delivery timing, use of rail rights-of-way for long distance telephone lines, use of rights-of-way for temporary material storage, and passes for inspectors and other personnel. General agreements had been struck years ago in all these areas, however regular adjustments had been necessary to reflect evolving conditions. In this particular meeting, the main change negotiated is the increase in space for temporary storage in exchange for a wider delivery window. There had evidently been a pre-meeting amongst the railroad people, as they are all in agreement for the change, most only adding details on storage location relative to specific stations or grain elevators. Ultimately, everything goes smoothly enough for Lora to question the reason for her attendance. Since this is her first meeting though, she considers it prudent to reserve judgment until she has a chance to talk to Phillip.

On the way back to the yard, Phillip is contemplative. It is only at the halfway point that he opens his mouth.

"That went well," he says, furrowing his brow.

"I take it that the meetings are normally different?"

"Yes, very different."

Lora thinks back to Claude, the farmer she met on the train to Kralovna: "The railway people were more organized this time, like they are with the farmers?"

"Farmers deal with the elevator operators rather than the railroad itself, so it's a bit different. But, yes, far more organized. Which is good, it should reduce the hassles for shipments that use both inter-regional and regional lines."

"But it also means that the Committee is asserting control in a way that you haven't seen before."

"If it is the Committee. It could just be new department leadership."

"The woman who came in late, have you ever seen her before?"

"No, why?"

"She came in after introductions. I was wondering what her role was."

They arrive at the yard in time for lunch. With the possibility of more Committee presence and the question of how Maurice and Violet fit into things, she is happy to eat in relative silence – answering Anna's intermittent questions about the meeting with monosyllables – and pass the afternoon unloading crossbars. The fantasy of becoming someone who pulls the strings seems foolish to her, now that she has a fresh reminder of just how little she knows of government machinations. Phillip's belief that she had some special insight was flattering, but no more accurate than that of her control over the decision to send Maurice to prison.

Chapter 8

Léon wonders just how much Arria knew about Paetus' involvement in the coup against the emperor. He somehow doubts that the two of them discussed the idea at length, sitting at the kitchen table late into the night. Her efforts to stay near him only started after the rebellion fell apart and Paetus was captured, so it was unlikely that she had accompanied him on his plot-related travels before that point. Beyond the idea of a glorious death, she justified her desire to end her life at the same time as her husband by the long and happy life lived together. There were so many secrets on both sides though, that even together they were miles apart.

He strolls past the three black cars on his way to the café, nodding to the one inspector he recognizes, having occasionally had coffee with him in the past. When he woke up that morning, it came to him that the invertebrate table by the counter would be perfect for the day. Today he attempts to write something meaningful to Lora, to close the distance between them using without betraying the secrets they share. The idea goes counter to his usual approach of describing life without embellishment, but a challenge is not unwelcome.

Lora had sent a straightforward letter to Natalie and Eugenie, describing her new life. In Natalie's opinion, the letter was even more lifeless and impersonal than the first one, despite the 'I love and miss you all' at the end. After being exposed to the poetics of Pliny's letters, her expectations were perhaps a bit high. Lora's warmth came far more from her presence and the sensitivity with which she helped her daughters navigate the pitfalls of growing up than from her words themselves. For Eugenie, the important thing was that their mother sent the letter, showing that she was thinking of them, rather than what it said. Both girls immediately set about replying, but only Eugenie had the patience to finish and send something – an equally dry, fictionalized account of how things hadn't much changed since Lora left. She tried to maintain a balance between Lora leaving an unfillable hole in her existence, to underline how important her mother was to her, and the family continuing along without any real issues, to avoid making Lora feel guilty. She ended up erring on the side of saying that everything was okay, afraid that she might inadvertently reveal just how hellish school life had become.

Hervé brings a pot of lemon tea and pulls himself out a chair.

"I don't think that I have ever seen you at the invertebrate table before."

"I am trying to write something rather different, and I suspect that my subconscious has been hinting since I woke up this morning that this is the table where I can do it."

"Ah. Perhaps you would like a different tea. I shouldn't have presumed."

"The tea is fine for now, thank you." Léon waits for Hervé to say what he sat down to say, since he almost never sits uninvited at a table without something on his mind.

At the moment the tea has over-steeped the ideal amount for Léon's taste, Hervé sighs and says, "Lucien is in prison."

Lucien, an occasional contributor to the journal and infrequent participant in café discussions, is one of the more deliberate members of the community. He has always been conscious of the risks of his actions, and only follows through with those he deems worth the potential price. A sensible approach for those who do not have an obsessive need to put pen to paper and send that paper into the world, even a very constrained world, rather than putting it in a drawer.

"For how long?" Léon asks.

"Two years."

"That's really unfortunate. What was he convicted of?"

"Translating an official article for a foreign friend and commenting that it was anti-Semitic. And having the intention of publishing abroad, but the prosecutors didn't have much proof for that one."

"I imagine that it would be difficult to prove someone's intentions if they haven't acted on them yet."

"Still, two years. I enjoyed what he wrote. Not to mention that business suffers every time this sort of thing happens."

"It's the cost of your future glory, and maybe his too."

"That dream is the only thing keeping me going. Do you think he'll be okay?"

"Yeah, knowing him he's been preparing himself for this eventuality for years. It's the young ones, your fabled next generation, that wouldn't do so well. They just don't have a realistic grasp of consequences and don't realize that landing in prison more often than not does not lead to society changing for the better."

Léon's last sentence trails off as he stares in disbelief at Natalie, who is walking towards them from the rear of the café, pausing to glance at the writing on the tables she passes. Hervé looks back and forth between them a number of times before realizing what is happening. He rises nonchalantly from the table and redirects Natalie with a casual yet firm grip on her elbow to the fungus table, the table the least visible from the street, and then retreats to behind the counter. Léon sips his tea and contemplates his daughter, who is already absorbed by the poetics of molds and mushrooms. After recognizing the inevitability of this scene – it is hard to think of a forbidden fruit more enticing for an insatiable and curious reader than banned reading materials – he makes a quick trip to the washroom and then pulls up a chair across from his daughter.

"It's a good thing that what I say carries weight."

"It does, it's not as if I came in the front door."

"The police out front can see the side entrance perfectly well."

"There are police out front right now?"

"The three black cars."

"Oh," she shrugs, "it's too late now."

"You say that so casually. But what if it is not too late? What if you were able to take this decision back? It doesn't mean much of course, you still haven't had to suffer any real consequences, you would have to take my word that this is perhaps not a path you want to go down. And why would you take what I say seriously? What would stop you from making a similar choice tomorrow?"

"I don't want to go back. I don't want you to burn your journals just because you feel that you have to protect me. I want you to stop feeling you have to lie to me."

"That's just not going to work. In four or five years, perhaps, but not now."

"But why? Why do you want to keep me in the dark?"

"It would tear the family apart, and for practically nothing."

"Things are already coming apart, dad. Can't you see that?"

"I'll admit that things are not going as well as they could be."

Natalie does not dignify Léon's understatement with a response.

"Fine, we can work on changing things, but not here and not just between you and me. And, only on the condition that you do nothing so foolish as coming here in the future."

"Only if you let me read your books."

"Okay, but it will take a while to set that up."

"You don't have copies of your own books?"

"They are not easily accessible. Having them at hand would be a needless risk, which is a concept that you need to learn. Now, let's see how we are going to get you out of here."

Léon motions to Hervé to come over: "Hervé, can you get the girl out without her presence here listed on her record?"

Hervé cringes at Léon's impoliteness. He sits at the table and responds to Léon while looking at Natalie: "Yes, but can't she stay longer? The café feels younger already and she evidently appreciates poetry."

"Yeah," Natalie chimes in, emboldened by the support. "If you have your way, dad, I'll never be able to come back, and I've never seen anything like these tables."

"Léon." Hervé turns to look at his friend. "How can you possibly deprive Natalie of my café, and my café of her?"

"Stop," Léon orders, before asking, "Wait, how do you know her name?"

"Some people at this table are actually polite and introduce themselves," Hervé replies in a condescending tone. He then turns back to Natalie: "These tables are veritable works of art that very few people have the privilege of seeing, particularly people of your generation."

"Okay, that's enough," Léon says, once again finding himself in a conversation involving his daughters where he struggles to maintain some semblance of authority. "The longer Natalie is here, the harder it is going to be for her to leave without repercussions."

To his surprise, Natalie agrees: "The tables are really lovely, Hervé, but my dad is right. How am I going to get out of here?"

"I suppose," Hervé replies, disappointed that his first opportunity to show off his café is so brief. "Follow me."

Léon stays at the table while Natalie follows Hervé to the back. Hervé picks up a large sack of dirty linens and hands it to her.

"Congratulations, you have a new job. My laundryman, whose name is also Hervé, serves both legitimate and illegitimate clientele, including a member of the Committee. You are going to take the bag to his laundry, the address is on the tag, and tell him that I sent you and that you need a job. You'll be running around town for a while picking up dirty laundry. You should be followed to his place and then for a while after that. When they see where you are going, they won't write anything down immediately. Once you have shown that you work for him and have been sent to a couple of important places, they should let the surveillance drop. Given your father, it'll take some time. On the bright side, you'll earn some money and see parts of the city you've likely never been to before."

"Thanks, Hervé!" Natalie says, already heading for the door. "I won't forget about the tables."

Once she is gone, Hervé takes the pot of lemon tea abandoned at the invertebrate table, makes a fresh pot, and rejoins Léon.

"You have a lovely daughter," he says softly.

"I had hoped that she and her sister would have followed in their mother's footsteps. No, that's not true. I never hoped for anything, I wasn't that invested. I had expected that the girls would take after their mother because she was always there for them, because she was – and still is – completely invested."

"Are you disappointed?"

"No, of course not," Léon replies with a smile. "How can I be disappointed with a daughter who can admire a poem on the obscure ecological functionality of yeast?"

"I'll take that as a cue that you are done talking about your family."

"I really appreciate what you did for her."

"Well, we can't have people too young to fully grasp the extent of what they can lose actually lose everything simply because they have the good taste to visit my café."

With that, Hervé goes to serve another client. Léon, whose ideas are influenced as much by the table as by Natalie's visit and the news of Lucien's conviction, starts writing a feuilleton describing the evolution of his reactions to the news of fellow writers being sent to prison over the years.

Chapter 9

Lora is sitting on outdated exchanges with Anna and Maurice in the shade at the end of the yard, reflecting on the fact that she has yet to receive a letter from Léon. In the short time that she has been in Kralovna, the hours spent idly waiting for materials to arrive has become a regular part of the rhythm of her job. The department relies entirely on the railroads for long distance freight, and deliveries are rarely on time. She understands far better now than in the meeting with Phillip the need for more temporary storage along the tracks, but realizes just how insufficient the change will be. Given the primitive state of the roads in the region though, the department does not have much choice but to try to manage the problem as best it can.

The first time Lora lounged under the overhang on the exchanges – as much as one can lounge on big metal boxes covered with sockets and bulbs – Anna pointed out which ones they could use and which ones were off limits. Essentially, they had to keep to the 'hello girl' side, where all the local area operator-run exchanges were located, and avoid the automated and long distance machines. She explained that operators were, for as long as she could remember, called hello girls for fairly obvious reasons. As these sorts of experiences repeated themselves though, Anna had less and less to say. She would occasionally spontaneously offer an anecdote from her life on the farm and was always happy to explain an aspect of the telephone system at length when asked, but her stories had started to repeat themselves and Lora had fewer questions. Ultimately, the silence of Maurice and Lora was too obstinate to resist.

The three sit, lost in their own worlds, listening to the sounds of the city beyond the walls of the yard. Lora had received a letter from Eugenie that unsettled her. It was stiff and lacking in detail, very much against the character of someone so sensitive to the world around her, and particularly to anything negative. Eugenie always tried to shield her sister, all the while finding it impossible to shield herself, from the cynicism and anger of those around her. The letter read like the second note Lora sent, which Eugenie wouldn't have written even if she was hurt by Lora's terse words for fear of creating more unhappiness. The only reason for it is that she felt the need to protect her mother from what was really going on. Another Arria in the family, but without the skill that Arria had in hiding their son's passing from her husband while he was ill so as to avoid a shock that might have ended his life. Eugenie should not have to be in that position, but now that Lora is no longer near her there is no one to protect her. Anything could have happened.

The downtime in the yard is torture as Lora can't stop her imagination from running through the practically endless list of possibilities for what might be happening in the capital. The lack of letter from Léon only makes things worse. Rationally, she knows not to expect much from him. He separated his writing from his family life so long ago. She couldn't imagine how difficult it would be to put them back together, to write on subjects he had worked so hard to avoid, in a format so alien to him. Even after years of writing vacuous judgments, including just enough detail for the purpose at hand and adapting her style to ever-changing bureaucratic standards, writing letters to her family was challenging. It would have to be immeasurably worse for someone who writes freely using their own voice, who writes purposefully and with depth, to put something on paper that is only able to hint at what is important, that must avoid honesty and passion so as to not attract the attention of the inspectors who would undoubtedly read it. Knowing all this has no effect on her need to hear from her husband and to get even the smallest sense that everything is okay.

The great irony is that she can't reach her own family by telephone. While the system is open in this region to encourage its development by farmer syndicates, it is closed in the capital to people who are not in good standing with the Committee, even if that person is part of a family that in general has clean records and does not suffer any other adverse consequences. The official reason given is to prevent the organization of disruptive elements in society. The real reason is to hide endemic capacity shortages. In her previous life, Lora had overheard inspectors wishing that everyone had phones so they could eavesdrop on conversations from a convenient, central location.

"So, you have a piano?" Maurice asks Lora, noticing that she was becoming increasingly agitated and recognizing the frustration of someone imagining the worst and being powerless to know what is really occurring or being able to do something about it.

"Pardon?" Lora replies, coming out of her trance and realizing that she has been obsessively twisting a knob of the exchange she is sitting on.

Anna jumps on the possibility of an actual conversation and of learning something new about one of her coworkers: "You have a piano at home? Do you play?"

"No, I mean, yes, I have a piano. I don't play though. It was there when I moved in."

"Do you like music? Are you going to learn to play it?"

"I hadn't thought about it. I like music as much as anyone, I guess."

"Wait," Anna says, then turns to Maurice: "How did you know to ask about a piano?"

Maurice shrugs: "She mentioned it in passing one day, I don't really remember when."

Anna does not hide her suspicion that something more is going on, but decides that probing further is not worth the risk of Maurice and Lora retreating back into their shells. She continues. "I bet that the reason you remember the piano, Maurice, is because you play. You can teach Lora. That would be perfect."

Maurice is taken aback by the accuracy of Anna's logic. He mumbles, "Well, I used to play a bit, it's been a long time."

"On the farm, people would just pick up whatever instrument was around. The older folks all knew how to play something so they would teach the beginners, mainly when the family or the community got together. Nobody really practiced on their own and my mom was the only one who could read music. Everyone just sort of knew all the traditional songs already, so all they had to do was to figure out how to play them. Anyway, the point is that you don't have to be an expert to help Lora get started."

It is Lora's turn to notice that Maurice is starting to fidget, so she asks Anna, "Does music replace hockey for the summer?"

Before Anna has a chance to respond, Maurice exclaims, "Okay, yes, if Lora wants to learn how to play, I will give it a shot."

"Thanks, but I'm not interested," Lora replies, wondering what is motivating Maurice to talk, let alone offer to do something that he must know she cannot accept. It is simply unthinkable to invite someone who has been to prison to her place. She has envied Léon for a long time that he, and everyone else with a blemished record, does not really have to worry about such things. They have to worry about going too far, but having someone who the Committee decided needed some time in prison come to her place to teach her the basics of the piano, so long as the pieces taught were acceptable, would not be going too far.

Anna looks disappointed: "To be honest, I have no talent with music either. My mom tried to teach me, hoping that I had taken after her, but it was no use. I was relieved actually when she gave up. I made her proud in other ways."

"Such as?" Lora asks, once again trying to divert the topic away from the piano.

"I'm here. It doesn't seem like much – work on the farm was far more demanding – but we learned the hard way when my older brother wanted to go to university that farmers are not workers. The Committee tried to make us into workers fifteen-odd years ago, but there was a bad season, resources were diverted, and the plan was never put in place. They were not prepared for the feast or famine nature of wheat crops. Access to universities is skewed towards kids from working families though, so my brother didn't get in. The rules treat people as if they belong to two groups – workers and capital – they didn't even consider us. With less and less people needed to run the farm though, we can play that game; we can put up telephone lines, build roads and meet the official definition of a working family.

"Unfortunately, that means that we are scattered all over the place. I may be useless at playing an instrument, but I miss when the community was close enough to get together to play whenever we all had a free evening. I miss the hockey team, and I am pretty good at hockey. Occasionally, I will hear someone talk about the loneliness and isolation of the farmstead, but, at least for me, it feels far worse here. But my younger siblings and my kids, if I ever have kids, will be able to go to university if they want to, and that makes it worth it."

Lora represses the temptation to tell Anna all about her own situation, a situation that seems to be almost a mirror image. Instead she asks, "How do you keep in contact with your family?"

"I phone them and visit when I can. I take time off to help out at seeding and harvest. They come into town sometimes, for a treat. With all the distractions here, they can't imagine that I think of them at all."

The last words are shouted as two rail cars are slowly backed into the spur line. The first is empty, the second piled with spools of copper wire. A moment later, Phillip exits the administration building and goes to count the number of spools. The engineer unhooks the cars and speaks for a moment with Phillip before climbing back into the locomotive and driving off. Anna, Lora and Maurice approach Phillip, who is noting something on a pad in his hand.

"Are they good to unload?" Anna asks.

"Yeah, months late and less than half what was promised," Phillip grumbles before answering Anna, "Unload ten spools, the rest will be taken directly to the crew working on the northern line. Load up the other car with crossbars, it will be going to the same place."

The three start pulling the cranes to the cars as Phillip makes his way back to his war room. They take the spools off the train and load the crossbars at their usual, unhurried pace. They finish loading two thirds of the crossbars at quitting time, grateful to have some work queued up for the next day.

Lora wanders home, enjoying the sensation of her body not screaming its fatigue or hunger at her. She pauses to look down a street that blends into the prairie at the horizon and wonders how she could have been so uncomfortable with the openness of this new world. She also wonders how she could have gone so far in imagining the worst regarding her family. Back when she discussed this option with Léon, one of the conclusions they came to was that it would not work if they could not trust each other. She has to continue to believe that Léon is capable of handling the challenges of effectively being a single parent. Besides, Eugenie is a teenager; there is a wide variety of reasons for her to want to hide things from her mother that do not include the world coming to an end. For all the moral fatigue of being a judge in the capital, at least she was so overwhelmed with cases that she had relatively little time to reflect. She really needs a mechanism to deal with the intermittent hours of idleness and her mind's tendency to fixate on how things might be going wrong.

As soon as she arrives at her place, she sits at the piano and randomly taps the keys, eventually coming up with some simple melodies. The desire to become someone who pulls the strings comes back to her. Violet did not seem to have any concern with being with Maurice in public. If Lora could be in the same position, she would be able to ask Maurice to teach her to play without compromising herself or her daughters. This of course assumes that nothing else was at play in the café, an assumption that she can't reasonably make. Still, it is a more attractive possibility than to be like Léon, to have no concerns because everything is already compromised.

Chapter 10

Léon arrives home to find Eugenie at the kitchen table with a boy of about the same age. He tries to remember if he has seen the boy before, but he had never really paid much attention to his daughters' friends. It is, if he is not mistaken, fairly rare for the girls to invite friends to the house and his recollection does not do a great job in differentiating between those of Eugenie and those of Natalie. When Léon enters the kitchen, Eugenie says, "Natalie hasn't come home yet. Have you seen her?"

"Yes," Léon replies laconically, not inclined to go into any detail with someone he does not know in the room.

Eugenie picks up on the cue: "This is Albert, dad. He is a friend from school. You know his dad."

"My father is Lucien Fischer, Mr. Chaulieu," Albert explains, rising confidently to shake Lucien's hand.

Léon's mind whirls. His first thought is that now he knows that Eugenie decided to get to know other kids at school who were shunned rather than becoming cruel to them to prove to those whose families have clean records that she still belongs with them. From there, the manner by which she got her hands on the journal becomes clear. If she is so imprudent as to invite home the son of an imprisoned writer, someone who likely is himself familiar with clandestine publishing, there is no doubt that the police have noticed her. Natalie's visit to the café was difficult enough; this is impossible.

"It is nice to meet you, Albert," Léon manages to reply with an ordinary voice, deciding that there is no point in lying about his connection to Lucien. "I am sorry about your father."

"Thank you," Albert replies.

"I'm sorry that we lost your copy of the journal the other day," Léon says, fishing for more answers.

"I am not sure what you are referring to."

"Ah, I must be mistaken. Would you like to stay for dinner?"

"No thanks, I should go." Both Albert and Eugenie get up and she walks him to the door.

Léon wishes that he knew when Natalie would be coming home and he could start preparing dinner. He needs something to hide the awkwardness of the situation. Obviously the parental authority card – augmented by burning the journal – had not resulted in anything positive. He hadn't even had a chance to try the common decision made by equal and mature people approach that Natalie had agreed to earlier. He can still try that approach of course, there isn't really anything to lose at this point, but he doesn't see that there is much to gain either.

Eugenie comes back to the table and sits down without engaging her father in conversation.

"This is an interesting development," Léon opens.

"I followed the rules you set out," Eugenie replies, already on the defensive. "I have not touched anything you are involved in from your other life, nor have I left anything compromising around the house."

"Are you happy?"

Eugenie is at a loss for words, not at all expecting the question.

"I mean," Léon continues, "I know that you have been miserable at school since the police searched the house. Are things getting better?"

"Yes, but no thanks to you."

"Thanks to Albert?"

"He has ideals, he doesn't just skulk around in the shadows and lie to everyone."

"It's funny, I always pegged you as the reasonable one."

"What is the point of being reasonable? Albert's dad tried being reasonable and now he is in prison. Mom is trying to be reasonable, and she is stuck in the middle of nowhere."

"Your mother is in the middle of nowhere because she loves you and wants you to have a bright future. You know that, though; I've mentioned it before. Lucien, Albert's father, always made sure that the risks he took were justified. He believed that going to prison or, in your case, limiting one's future for no practical end was not worthwhile. Being reasonable in both cases simply means doing things for good reasons.

"I was hoping to have this conversation after your sister got home. If being around Albert makes you happy, I think that is great. You should be happy. Was it worth it to invite him here, though, and raise the possibility that the police will search the house again, or worse? If you act on his ideals, will you be doing something that makes life better on the ground, or…"

At that moment Natalie enters the house, visibly tired. She shuffles into the kitchen and slumps down on a chair.

"Picking up dirty laundry is hard," she groans.

"What were you doing picking up dirty laundry?" Eugenie asks, surprised.

"New job. Dad can explain."

"And here is a case in point," Léon says. He explains Natalie's visit to the café and how risking a tarnished record for so little is not reasonable. "As both of you have found out, the risks each of us take have repercussions for the whole family. So, since it is evident that none of us wants take the easy route of staying on the good side of the Committee, I suggest that we decide together what the limits should be and how we can support each other."

"Can we do this tomorrow?" Natalie pleads.

Léon looks at Eugenie, who nods.

He goes to the counter to make a quick, cold dinner. Eugenie joins him, as she has come to habitually do. He is slicing tomatoes when Eugenie lightly elbows him and points to Natalie, who has fallen asleep at the table. They stop to carry her upstairs and put her in bed. The fatigue is contagious, sapping Léon's and Eugenie's desire to continue their conversation about Albert. They eat slowly and quietly and then turn in.

* * *

The next day, Léon is the first one home. He finished the feuilleton on his reactions to the imprisonment of writers over the years and has tried to turn back to the still unwritten letter to Lora. His mind does not cooperate though, instead recalling the sensation of freedom spending evenings with fellow creative types who were banished from the official record. He hasn't visited the café in the evening or gone to a party since the serious discussion began with Lora about her taking a different direction to keep the family on the Committee's good side. Although in certain ways writing and frequenting other people in a similar situation are inseparable – his preferred subject is after all the daily realities of a writer of banned works – the evenings were never central to who he is. Regardless of how much continuing to write articles and putting out the journal, along with his continued presence at the café where he does the work, may undermine the project they decided on and the sacrifice Lora was willing to make, there was never any question of stopping. Lora certainly would have never condoned it. There was in fact never a question of stopping anything, since nothing Léon did was reckless. At the same time, everything carried a risk and it was not exactly difficult to simply stop seeing his more or less colleagues, so that is what happened. He doesn't remember making a conscious choice, it just fit in naturally to what he and Lora were trying to accomplish. In writing his article, and listening to snippets of community news from Hervé, he feels very isolated.

Eugenie and Natalie enter the house together and head directly to the bathroom, then upstairs where Eugenie changes her clothes. When the girls finally enter the kitchen, Léon can see that Eugenie has been roughed up, with bruising on her arms.

"What happened?" Léon asks.

"The police picked up Albert," Eugenie responds, becoming

increasingly angry as she speaks. "They are bullies. We were sitting outside school, talking, and they drove up. Three of them got out the car and jumped him. They restrained him and dragged him to the car. It was only when he was in handcuffs that they bothered telling him that they were bringing him in for questioning. It all happened so fast. One of them was sitting on his back, I tried to pull him off, another one grabbed me and shoved me back against the wall. Then they were gone."

Natalie interjects. "That's how I found her, completely out of it, sitting against the wall."

"Where did they take him?" Eugenie asks her father desperately. "What are they going to do to him?"

"Chances are, not very much. The investigators who run the interrogations are generally very polite and friendly. They will ask him questions on all sorts of topics for up to a week, and then let him go. If he is as wise as his father, he won't say much and little will be added to his file. If he is too blinded by his ideals, he may betray what he is thinking. Whatever is added to the file will be used to send him to prison whenever the Committee feels that the time is right. Everyone is guilty, but it helps to record the specifics."

Eugenie puts her head in her hands and does not respond.

"Has he done anything that would bring him to their attention?"

"No," Eugenie replies with conviction, before admitting under her breath, "I don't know. He had just started a school newspaper, but it was all fluff approved by the faculty sponsor. He gave me that copy of the journal, but then why wasn't I taken in? Maybe someone overheard him saying something, maybe he's been doing things I don't know about." Her voice trails off.

"However you feel about it, I am grateful that they did not take you in."

"Why?" Eugenie lifts her head to look at her father in his eyes. "Do you think that I would say something, be blinded by my ideals?"

"It's not that, although I don't think that anyone can really predict how they would react in those sorts of situations. No, it's simply that I am grateful that you did not have to go through it. As it happens, I am also relieved that it is not too late to have the conversation we talked about yesterday, if you feel up to it, of course."

"Now you are going to say that being around Albert is too much of a risk."

"Well, no, not necessarily. Ultimately, that is up to you to decide, but hopefully we can agree to certain things as a family. However, given what has happened today, maybe we need to put it off one more day."

"That's not fair," Natalie cries, "at this rate I will never be able to read your books."

"You want to read dad's books?" Eugenie asks, surprised.

"Don't you?"

"I, I can't say that I've thought about it." Eugenie looks at her sister's pleading eyes and says to her father, "I'm okay, we can talk now."

Léon tries to start things off in the same way that Lora had with him by defining long term goals and then figuring out how to meet them in an acceptable and realistic manner. This quickly falls apart as neither Eugenie nor Natalie have a solid idea of what they want in the distant future. They settle on two somewhat contradictory objectives for the girls: that they generally avoid anything that might hinder their graduation from high school and the possibility of attending university, and that they do not let societal rules force them to live a lie. As for Léon, he has in a way already achieved his goal of writing and releasing that writing in the world, even the realization of the goal is a pale echo of his beginnings as a well-respected novelist. His role, then, is to try to be a better father, though as far as he can tell, that just means muddling along, helping when he can and accepting that his daughters are going to ignore any hard limits he tries to impose if they think that the limits are unreasonable or hypocritical.

Practically, the only things that change regard bringing his two worlds closer together. He moves his old novels to the library locker and gets into the habit of keeping one on him most of the time, in addition to his notebook. In the evenings, he gives the book to Natalie to read and she hands it back to him at the end of the night. Essentially, Léon being in possession of his own book is not illegal, but distributing it is, so the time it is in Natalie's hands is limited to when she can actually read it in private. The journal is more complicated, as it is a compilation of feuilletons, poems and the like written by different authors. On the other hand, distribution is technically not illegal since the pieces have never been banned. The problem is that they could be banned in the future, so he agrees to type up an extra copy for the house, with the understanding that it disappears as soon as it has been read.

Léon finds bringing the two worlds together surprisingly easy since the incidents with Natalie at the café and Eugenie with the journal. He feels that the battle is lost; the girls know more or less what he does and have on the whole taken it remarkably well. He just hopes to guide them as best he can so their long term happiness is not ruined. The main concern is whether Eugenie will hold to what they agreed to when Albert is back at school. Ironically, it was undoubtedly Albert who gave her the strength to get through the dark days at school and ultimately accept what Léon had done. He is certainly relieved that she no longer cries herself to sleep. On the other hand, it is clear that she doesn't believe that he goes far enough in working against the rules of the Committee. He suspects that Lucien had endeavored to show Albert the wisdom of being careful and meticulous, and of not taking unnecessary risks. When he went to prison though, Albert likely rejected his father's approach, thinking that if prison was inevitable, he might as well act brazenly and make the conflict as visible as possible to everyone. It is that route that Léon dreads for Eugenie.

Chapter 11

Lora realizes that, regardless of how many times she tells herself to trust Léon and that everything is okay in the capital, she will not have peace of mind until she knows for sure. As it is another idle day and she doesn't want to risk overthinking things, she leaves Anna and Maurice in the hello girl section and heads into the administration building to ask Phillip for some time off to see her family.

"Of course," Phillip responds. "To be honest, I am surprised that it has taken this long for you to ask. Most people fresh from the capital feel homesick pretty quickly and go back – some permanently – whether we authorize it or not."

"Thank you," Lora replies, already feeling more hopeful than she has been since Eugenie's letter.

As she turns to leave, Phillip calls, "Wait, I actually have a better idea. Why don't we treat this as a work trip? There are a couple of meetings that we are supposed to attend in the capital. It is just updates on ongoing projects and information sharing, no decision making or anything along those lines. All you would have to do is take notes and do up some summaries for me. You would have to leave today though, since the first meeting is tomorrow morning."

Lora nods, content to have an official reason for her trip. Phillip shuffles through the paper on the table until he finds an inspector's annual rail pass and several letters containing meeting details. He hands the pile of paper to Lora, wishes her a good trip and asks her to mention it to Anna before she leaves. Then he heads off to the exchange building across the street for a meeting of his own.

When Lora arrives in the capital, she exits the station's grey tunnel into the fading light of the day. She is both famished and numb from boredom, having been too hasty in her preparations to bring food or distractions. She had neither Claude nor Pliny to keep her company. Both the station and the streets around it are inundated by a sea of people who are so unanimated that they don't seem fully human. She makes her way through them, conscious of how closed in the area is. She glances down side streets and notices that all of them turn or end abruptly after several blocks; it is one aspect of the capital that she without a doubt prefers, even if the openness of Kralovna and the prairies does not bother her as much as it once did.

Lora heads straight home. The crowd thins as she gets further from the station and she notices the tell-tale three black cars behind her. It is unclear to her whether they are following her or not, but they put her on edge regardless. Her destination is obvious though and there is no point in thinking about the state of things until she gets there, so she decides that there is no point in doing anything other than continuing. Six blocks later, she glances back and the cars are gone. She takes a deep breath and wills herself to stop being anxious about all this, she hasn't been gone for very long and things like the three black cars and crowds of silent people are typical in the capital.

She enters the house quietly but, once the door is closed, calls out "I'm home." Eugenie comes running from the kitchen and Natalie from the living room, both exclaiming "Mom!" and hugging her tightly. Léon exits the kitchen slowly and hangs back, reverting automatically to the distance he was able to maintain before his wife left. Neither Eugenie nor Natalie reverts back though; while they are definitely effusive in expressing how much they miss their mother, they do not seem to be in any hurry to recount what has happened since she left. Overwhelmed by the happiness of seeing that everyone is alright, Lora does not immediately notice the change. It is only in seeing one of Léon's books in Natalie's hand that the idyllic scene starts to slip away from her.

"Natalie, what is that in your hand?" Lora asks, not trusting her first glance.

Natalie looks back at her father and then, after checking the page she is on, hands the book to her mother.

"There are perhaps certain things that we should discuss," Léon points out.

"It does seem that way," Lora replies, "but first, I am famished. I suppose that you have already eaten."

"We'll whip something up."

Lora hands the book back to Natalie, who returns to the living room. The three others go into the kitchen, where Lora receives her second surprise in seeing Eugenie join Léon at the counter to prepare her some food. She had thought that Eugenie would replace her in certain ways, particularly in being there for Natalie, but did not predict that she would take on roles that she herself avoided for the most part. She sits in her usual place at the kitchen table, beside a pile of papers that she chooses to ignore for the moment, and starts talking to fill the silence.

"I am in town for a couple of days on business. I didn't think of bringing a book for the trip here. The trip out would have been excruciating had you not thought of giving me Pliny's *Letters*, Léon. Everything is flat and straight out east; it seems to go on forever. Even in Kralovna, it is like that..."

Once the meal is prepared and Lora has finished eating, she asks what has happened since she left. Léon calls Natalie so that the whole family is sitting around the table, and then launches into the sequence of events that led Eugenie, Natalie and him to where they are now. Lora is floored, both by the story and by the fact that Léon was being so open with the girls at the table.

"It is a lot to absorb, I know," Léon concludes.

The three of them wait to hear Lora's reaction, which is slow in coming. In a way, she is not surprised by how things have turned out. The family's stability always rested on a delicate balance between her and Léon. As Léon is regularly under surveillance and it was common knowledge that Lora was being transferred, the police action as soon as she was gone was likely seen as a useful warning to not start using the house for other activities. And everything else largely cascaded from that. Certainly, Eugenie's and Natalie's futures are less assured than before, but they now have a more active role in shaping them. They are no longer in the dark and so have a place at the table. What she can't quite figure out what that means going forward. She doesn't even know if the delicate balance still exists.

"Yes," she finally replies, "it is a lot to take in, and I am not sure what to say. I have such mixed feelings about it all: I am really happy to see how much you," she looks at each of her daughters, "have grown. At the same time, I am so sorry that you have had to go through all this and have had to make such difficult choices. You are still so young."

"We are not so young anymore," Natalie points out.

"I am sorry, too. We have made your situation so much harder; you went to Kralovna to help ensure that we would be able get into university and live whatever life we would want in the future," Eugenie says.

"None of what has happened is your fault; you haven't ruined anything. Had I not gone, none of this would have happened, but who could predict that? And who knows what would have happened had I stayed? I think it would have been worse; being a judge is very political, and when the winds change in the Committee, they are one of the first groups to be sacrificed; but we can never know for sure. So, we do the best we can, which is exactly what you did. Besides, whatever life you want to live is quite broad – the university may not be in your future – and I want you to know that I will always try to be supportive."

The conversation continues along these lines, with Lora easing the anxiety of her daughters with insights into their situation mixed with comforting platitudes. Although the entire family is at the table, once Léon finished the initial explanation, he found himself excluded from the conversation. Although some of the

'I's, generalizations and contradictions that Lora uses irritates him slightly, he is just as happy to not be part of making Eugenie and Natalie feel better about their choices. Part of what has happened is their fault, the direct consequences of their choices. In his opinion they should recognize that, not to feel guilty about it, but to learn from it and hopefully make better choices next time.

The irritation is in part due to the fact that Lora will be gone in a day or two and so will not have to live directly with the fallout of their daughters' actions. He has the impression that she still sees the family dynamic as it once was, with him having the obligation to keep a certain distance so as not to risk sullying the domestic world with his other existence and her taking on most of the parenting responsibilities. He does not feel that it is the right moment to go into all this yet staying silent is not as easy as before, so he excuses himself and leaves the house.

Lora speaks as much for herself as for her daughters in saying that it is not their fault. She was not there; the pre-emptive decision to leave the judiciary before the Committee found it convenient to arrest her and to take a job as a worker far from the political heart of the country was motivated by her drive to not have her daughters denied education and other prospects. It was a decision to not abandon them, and yet she abandoned them anyway. She has to believe that it was nonetheless the right decision, regardless of the ultimate outcome. In that way, she envies Arria her clear and unshakeable conviction of what is best for her family.

After Léon has left, there is a moment when everything seems like before, with Lora and the girls together, chatting about everyday topics, and Léon distant, present but not close enough to feel like an integral part of the family. When Natalie came to the table though, she brought her father's novel and it sits there, incongruous with the nostalgia, pulling Lora back into the present. This in addition to the stack of papers between her and

Eugenie, papers that could simply be homework, but under the circumstances she wasn't so sure. She asks Natalie, "How do you find your father's book?"

"It's weird and complicated; very hard to read. Everything else I have read, the sentences just pull you further into the story, so long as they aren't too awkward or badly written. With dad's book, it is like you can take every sentence out and treat it as a poem, independent from the story. I keep rereading them that way and then losing where the story is going. And since the plot is not exactly straightforward to begin with, I have to read everything again and try not to be drawn in by the poetry. Have you read it?"

Eugenie starts to pay more attention to the papers than to the discussion, marking up the content.

"A long time ago, when it was available in bookstores," Lora replies, pretending to ignore Eugenie's change of focus.

"That is something I can't figure out, why was it banned?"

"I don't know the specifics. In general, works are banned because they express an opinion incompatible with social harmony."

"Yeah, that's what they say at school. But I don't see it. I have to finish it first though; maybe at the end rocketman turns out to be an anarchist or a fascist or something."

"It could also be your father's take on the world as a complex, chaotic place without easy answers."

"Huh, that would be stupid, so I guess it makes sense."

"I think we should ask what your sister is up to."

"Oh she's just editing articles for the paper."

"She's what?" Lora exclaims, surprised that Eugenie would do anything resembling school work beyond what was assigned of her own free will.

"It's just something for her boyfriend," Natalie adds.

Eugenie looks up, face reddening: "He is not my boyfriend."

"Who is he?" Lora asks.

"He is the editor of the school newspaper, which he just got started," Eugenie explains, consciously avoiding saying his name and unconsciously touching the fading bruises under her shirt. "He was picked up for questioning and nobody else is willing to step in. It is only the second issue and I don't want it to fail just because the police are harassing him." She sighs and leans back in her chair before continuing, "But I get your shock, I am terrible at this. I hope dad comes back soon."

Lora's surprise hits a new level: this is the first time she has heard one of her daughters say that they want their father around outside of the context of food and other household issues. She suppresses her concern about how close Eugenie is to someone the police harass, since it cuts awfully close to Léon, as well as the desire to suggest replacing 'the police' with 'the Committee', following the prairie way of thinking.

"I can help you if you would like," Lora offers.

"No thanks, I'll just wait for dad."

"Okay," she replies, making an effort to keep the mix of dejection and happiness out of her voice.

By this time, Natalie's nose is back in her book and the conversation dies. Lora contemplates her daughters and feels content. She stops speculating about whether they would be better off had she stayed and accepts the state of things. They are healthy, still in school, engaged in what could be considered productive pursuits. The family is closer to the edge than it has been in a long time, when Léon's books were first banned, but also healthier now that there aren't so many secrets between them. It is next to impossible to find out whether their records are still clean, but the fact that the police have not searched to the house since immediately after she left, that there was no visible surveillance of the house and that Eugenie was not picked up at the same time as the editor, indicates that their future is still open. Knowing this will make it much easier to survive the idle moments in the hello girl corner of the yard.

It also fuels the idea that she could go further, take more risks. Despite the role of powerless placeholder for the Department of Telephones that Phillip has set up for her for the meetings tomorrow, she might be able to get something else out of them.

Chapter 12

As soon as he has left the house, Léon decides to go to the café to indulge in an evening with other creative types. He finds a spot at the dinosaur/bird table, in front of a poem about a struthiomimus, almost completely undecipherable due to the number of scientific terms used. The table is generally lively, frequented mostly by musicians, librettists, songwriters and the like. Hervé had taken great pride in attracting that group to his establishment. It of course goes without saying that none of these people can officially call themselves any of the above, as none of them have the appropriate licenses or guild memberships.

Léon knows everyone at the table somewhat but none very well. Agatha, a violist and occasional member of several bands, is in the middle of explaining how the regular members of one of her groups had just been arrested. She wasn't present at the rehearsal the police raided, but the experience had become common enough that everyone could fill in the blanks with their own experiences. After a moment of sympathetic silence, she asks Léon:

"Hey, your wife is Lora right? Used to be a judge, now lives in Kralovna?"

"Yes," Léon replies with some hesitation, since even if this world is slowly invading his family life, he would still prefer that his family is not mentioned here. "Why?"

"Do you know Maurice Butterfield?"

"I've heard the name, a pianist, right?"

"Only one of the best pianists left in the country."

"Which isn't saying much," Etienne, a folk guitarist and songwriter, interjects.

"Right, anyway," Agatha continues, finding Etienne's remark needlessly cynical so early in the evening, "his interpretations of Ravel were brilliant, but he hasn't played much since he got out of prison. I have it on good authority that he works at the same place as your wife."

When Agatha says 'good authority', she glances at a woman at the conifer table by the window who seems to be having a light hearted conversation with a couple of poets. Léon looks over to see the only person in the room he can swear to have never met before. He asks Agatha who she is.

"Oh, that is Violet. I've seen her in here several times, started coming about the time that you stopped. She and Maurice go way back, that's all I really know. Really nice though."

It is difficult for Léon to be suspicious of anyone who takes the risk to be here and is accepted by the regulars. At the same time, he is inherently wary of anyone he doesn't know talking about his family. He makes a mental note to ask Hervé about the woman later.

"You're right, it has been a long time since I have been here," Léon says, smiling while changing the subject. "Has anything interesting happened since then?"

"My day job is with the transit authority, in maintenance," Etienne starts. "Our fleet of vehicles, a bunch of vans, have been falling apart for quite some time. A couple of months ago, someone finally noticed that major onsite repairs weren't being done. We had started using our cars and whatever else we could get our hands on, and so couldn't carry any of the big equipment. We grabbed a bus twice, unbolting and leaving the seats in the garage and stuffing it with what we needed, but the mechanics caught on the second time and now we don't have access to them.

"Anyway, someone higher up finally noticed and decided that something needed to be done. They went to the state car company, who refused flat-out to build vans, saying that the Committee priority was passenger vehicles and that they did not have the capacity to do both. So, they went abroad and got a bunch of vehicles imported. Which is great, but they didn't check their dimensions before they bought them. The transit garages have three bay sizes, for both maintenance and loading; one for the tram cars, one for the buses and one for the maintenance vehicles. The third was an afterthought, so barely fit the vans we used to have, and the new vans are much larger. We could have used the bus bays, but since the incidents I just mentioned, we have not exactly been on good terms with them.

"Now the person who got us the vans, which can't just be taken back, would have gotten our bays enlarged, which isn't that big a deal, but since the screw-up they were moved to who knows where in the administration. The replacement won't touch this with a ten foot pole because they are too scared to ask for the money; putting it as a line item in their budget will connect them to the mistake and they haven't been in the system long enough to be comfortable hiding the costs elsewhere.

"And that, my friends, is why I love my job."

"I just received a royalty check from the agency in the mail," says Flora, who is a jazz drummer whenever the opportunity to play presents itself. "The money was from abroad. I haven't gotten one of those in years. A few days later, I got a tax bill for most of it but there was still enough to regale myself tonight."

Hervé arrives at the table, as if on cue, apologizes for not being there earlier, takes orders, and then drifts away.

"Wow," Léon remarks, "that is quite a lot of cynicism in your interesting stories. I thought that we tried to leave that at the door."

"I'm sorry," Agatha responds, "but with so many arrests, Lucien already in prison, and, well, the list is too long and depressing, we are a bit off our game."

"We just can't get a break," Flora adds. "Even Etienne's jokes fall flat these days."

"I was worried that I was losing my touch," Etienne says. "Our world going to shit is far better."

Hervé comes back with the drinks and, at the same moment, Charles, a mathematician, pulls up a chair.

"People are really dispirited tonight."

"It is no better here," Agatha points out.

"Just as well. There are some thoughts floating around about formalizing our position against the Committee. We need to do more than just playing music and writing feuilletons, hunkered down and hoping things get better. Dispirited is just about the right mood to think about that sort of thing."

"That sounds brilliant," Etienne says with enthusiasm. "After all, they can't put us all in prison."

"Sure they could; building prisons is a great make-work project," Flora notes. "Seriously though, keeping to the shadows isn't really helping us."

"It really isn't," Agatha confirms.

"And you, Léon?" Charles asks.

"It is probably necessary, but I couldn't be a part of it."

"I would have thought that with the obstinacy with which you put out your journal, a journal that the authorities know well, you would be first in line to put form to our positions and get them out there."

"What are you thinking, specifically?" Agatha asks, touched by Léon's reticence.

"We are too early for specifics, but it would probably be around the human rights clauses in the constitution. It would have to be something solid at any rate, not just our opinions."

"We need to go international with it, the UN maybe," Etienne suggests.

"Sure, but Léon, why doesn't this interest you? No pressure or anything, it's not as if anyone has done anything yet, I'm just curious. Maybe you have some better ideas."

"No, it is a good idea and I can't think of anything better that fits with our values," Léon admits. "For me though, I just want to write what I write, put out the journal, live in relative peace and quiet. And if, by sticking to that, no more barriers are put up between my family and their happiness, so much the better."

"Fair enough, I think we can all respect that."

"It is easier when you don't have a family," Flora says.

"Or if one's family is already blacklisted," Agatha adds.

"So, I think that I will leave you guys to your plotting and scheming, and talk to Hervé for a moment." Léon takes his drink and heads to the counter, where Hervé is chopping lemons into wedges.

"You have lemons, that's a treat."

"That's just the tip of the iceberg; I also have limes."

"This is turning into a high-class joint."

"And it is lost on you starving artist types."

"You will be shocked to know that I am having an influence on your fabled next generation."

"Because your daughters forced your hand?"

"Because my daughters forced my hand. Still, earlier this evening I was helping to put together an issue of a school newspaper."

"And, I hear, letting someone read your old books." At the surprised look Léon gives him, Hervé explains: "She was back to pick up another load of dirty linens. Can't have her only come here once."

Léon nods, relaxing: "The challenge will be when she finishes with them."

"I'm sure we can arrange something to give her access to more books, without of course adding much risk."

"And I just left a table where there was plotting going on…"

"Do you mean the charter?"

"That wasn't the term used, but I imagine so."

"I would call it the opposite of plotting; it is more putting aside all our usual machinations for an instant to tell the Committee plainly and clearly that what they are doing is wrong."

"Ah, giving them words to hang us with."

"Oh, they'll find some way to hang us at some point anyway.

Everyone is guilty, haven't you heard."

"On occasion, and I have also heard once or twice that everyone has something to lose."

"As the proprietor of an elegant and tasteful café, I might think that that applies to me. But having something to lose does not mean that one should pass up the opportunity to take a stand against a bully, or the opportunity to open up the world of certain members of the younger generation. Elegant and tasteful, I have found, do not come without taking chances."

"And wisdom, too. To change the subject slightly, who is the woman at the conifer table? I have never seen her in here."

"Ah, Violet, the mechanical woman. A wheel deep in the government machine. Also very pleasant, has seen every corner of the country, soft spot for the avant-garde. I don't think that I have ever heard her express an opinion."

"Why does she come here? Isn't that a risk for someone higher up in the government?"

"I imagine that she comes in for the atmosphere and the lime wedges."

"And not to report back what is said?"

"The upside of having so many people go to prison over the years is that we have a good idea of where the evidence and accusations come from. That's a lie, actually; we just know where they don't come from. I know that you don't like talking about your family, but it was pretty obvious that your wife never told the authorities anything about this place you might have mentioned to her when she was a judge. Violet is no different."

"The Committee plays a long game though."

"Yes they do, and I could be wrong about a lot of people. But I can't run this café and distrust everyone at the same time."

"Yeah, you're right. Yet regarding my family; it makes me uneasy how much she might know about them."

"Personal details?"

"No, just who my wife works with."

"That bothers you?"

"She's no longer a judge."

"I am afraid that that is going to follow her for a long time to come, especially with this crowd. Still, I'll keep an ear out for anything else that might circulate in that vein. Another drink?"

"Alas, no. I have to get back to editing the newspaper of the next generation."

"I am very pleased that you decided to come for a visit. You should come more often."

"You already see me multiple times a week."

"That's not the same."

Léon passes by the dinosaur/bird table to say his goodbyes and exits the café. One of the black cars across the street is haloed by a streetlight; the other two are lost in the darkness of the evening. He enters the house to find that Eugenie has abandoned the newspaper articles scattered across the kitchen table and has retreated to her bedroom. Natalie and Lora are in the living room; the first still making her way through his novel with a furrowed brow, the second, half asleep, going through the papers Phillip gave her. He calls up to Eugenie that he is home, and she comes down quickly, determined to finish editing the articles and setting up a basic layout before the evening is over.

A couple of hours later, Léon joins Lora in bed. He recounts the events at the café in passing. At the mention of Violet and Maurice Butterfield, Lora sits up with a jolt. She listens intently and asks questions until she is satisfied that he has told her everything he knows. Her focus does not follow when he moves on to describing the idea of what Hervé referred to as the charter, so he stops talking without going into his reservations. Lora lies back down, turned towards her edge of the bed as Léon turns off his lamp and stares at the ceiling. Each is aware that the other is awake, yet no closer than had they drifted off their own exclusive dream world.

Chapter 13

The next morning, Lora stands at the edge of the kitchen, intimi-dated, watching Eugenie and Natalie move fluidly around each other, taking a bite of toast and a sip of coffee, stuffing a snack in their bags already packed with a miscellany of objects for school and personal use. Eugenie segues smoothly to the table to pick up the neat pile of articles left from the night before, and then, after a 'bye mom' and 'bye dad', they are gone. Lora can barely imagine the time not so long ago when she felt comfortable weaving around her daughters in such a small space. She tries to convince herself, without much success, that this is just another example of how she is no longer as central to the family as she once was and adds another justification to be more ambitious. She knows that her role is diminished, however she could not bring herself to join Léon at the table and watch the dance with detachment. She pours a cup of coffee and thinks of Violet. After what Léon told her last night, the very thought of someone who can attend meetings between government departments as freely as she dines with an ex-con pianist and frequents a café full of underground writers motivates her to do more. 'More' is still vague in her mind, but she has in any case a job to do for Phillip, so she contents herself for the moment with looking out for opportunities. With that, she kisses Léon distractedly and heads to the government quarter.

The government quarter houses the vast majority of the administration in buildings that are intended to exude strength and power but come off as dreary and unimaginative. Essentially they are a series of identical buildings that resemble the library – squat structures with heavy, concrete facades – following a wide boulevard up to the ornate government house, a building that predates the regime. The major difference between these buildings and the library is that they are painted white, a color that increases heat build-up along a street that has few trees or other shade. This goes some way in explaining the hurried gait of bureaucrats walking between buildings during the summer along otherwise abandoned sidewalks. The court of first instance, where Lora was a judge, is the third building on the left, a location that makes very clear that the judiciary is not independent.

Lora has a certain nostalgia for the place and her former position in it, even though she can't explain exactly why. Perhaps it was because it was so near to the center, where countless important decisions are made. That makes no sense to her though, since she was never privy to the decisions in their entirety, let alone able to influence them. She was just one more worker on the assembly line, doing her small part in the creation of a product to be sold as justice, ignorant of the details of the other components and how they all fit together. Only it was worse, because people who actually did work on an assembly line were more respected and had more opportunities available to them and their families. She lives a life closer to the central philosophy of the Committee and to the ideals of society in Kralovna, working in the yard, even if both the philosophy and the ideals assume a level of contentment that continues to elude her. Still, despite knowing all of this, the feeling of nostalgia does not fade.

Phillip had accurately described the meetings; he had undoubtedly attended them in the past. They were just large enough, about thirty to forty people, to blend into the background. Lora takes copious notes without concerning herself with the relevance of what she was hearing and never contributes to the general conversation. When other invitees speak with her, she limits details about herself to a bare minimum, copying Violet's style by replacing details with anecdotes that seem personal but actually say very little about her. She runs into the same difficulty as in the café in Kralovna with Maurice and Violet; unlike Violet, she does not have a seemingly inexhaustible store of experiences to draw from. By the end of the day, her stories about the piano in her apartment and the goulash at the café are worn thin. Lora does see Violet, or someone she takes to be Violet, in the distance one time between meetings, but she is absent from the meetings themselves.

Lora takes copious notes because she wants to be seen as reacting to everything she hears in the same way, in addition to not being entirely sure what might be useful for Phillip or her own project. At the same time, she sees the potential in two areas. The first regards road rights-of-way. Up until now, she has taken for granted that outside of urban areas, the rights-of-way useful to the Department of Telephones are of the railway variety. The pertinent meeting is essentially a presentation by the Department of Public Works, the department that oversees government, which is to say non-local, roads. They present an aggressive plan for inter-regional road development and an associated program to promote cars and trucks as complementary modes to the train for long distance freight and passenger movement. From her experience in the yard and attending the meeting with the railroad executives, it is obvious that the rail bottleneck is one of the most significant limitations in the expansion and improvement of the telephone network. If roads were to be sufficiently upgraded, materials could be sent to crews far more efficiently and more direct routes could be opened up along which lines could be run. There are significant limitations to a shift to roads, with a system of almost 50,000 poles already existing in rail rights-of-way and shipments from suppliers to the yard generally too large to be taken by truck. Nonetheless, Lora indicates in her notes that this plan has potential.

The second meeting that interests her is a discussion led by the Department of Municipal Affairs on the inability of municipalities to provide basic services needing a high level of capital investment. The conversation focuses largely on sanitary and electrical systems, but most of the ideas can be applied to the telephone. A number of telephone exchanges on the prairies are run by the towns in which they are installed. With more and more farmer syndicates connecting to the system though, it is increasingly difficult for them to upgrade the exchanges and other centralized equipment in a timely manner. Even in the capital, the lack of capacity for new telephone lines is to a great extent due to parts of the system being controlled locally, a holdover from before long distance lines became a reality. The Department of Telephones regulates all the exchanges, and has a rule in place regarding level of service; but the rule is useless without coordinated investment. Centralized management of the exchanges – while leaving the rural areas with their independence – would likely save money through bulk purchases of upgraded machines and would allow more money to be targeted towards weak spots in the network.

Lora has more difficulty in imagining how other projects can help improve the Department of Telephones' system. To Lora's way of thinking, improvements to the system are a crucial means to her personal end. Phillip and everyone else raised on the prairies are primarily concerned with practical developments, so that has to be her focus. The Committee on the other hand is more concerned with maintaining normalcy, in form if not in substance. In order to influence the choices of the department while avoiding the spotlight, she has to start with giving Phillip advice that is both pragmatic and that endears her, or is at the very least neutral, to people in the capital. From there, hopefully she can gain sufficient immunity to not have to worry about the adverse consequences of taking Maurice up on his offer to teach her how to play the piano, among other things.

Continuing to follow what she sees as Violet's method, Lora seeks out people it would be good to know. She is still driven by her deep seated trepidation of frequenting the wrong sort of people though, which results in a misunderstanding about how

Violet acts. Lora does not pick up on an important part of what Léon had told her, that Violet had been involved in the underground scene off and on for enough time for people to be comfortable with her, which, with the current of distrust running through society, means that she had been there for quite some time. She is in a sense like Hervé the laundryman, someone who works with both sides and is accepted by both sides, not only because he is good at what he does, but also because he is not prone to being open about his opinions, assuming of course that he has many opinions to begin with. For the two, the notion of people it would be good to know, along with that of sufficient immunity, is strange because everyone is good to know and there is no magic moment when they can start doing things with people like Maurice. It then becomes a question of how other people react to them. Individuals who use others in underhanded and destructive ways tend to move on once they find that they have no leverage. People in positions of power respect them as they are engaging, effective and never broach awkward topics. People like Maurice are very similar to those in power, particularly in regards to respecting their discretion, while appreciating the fact that they do not abandon them in difficult times.

Lora does however get to know representatives of the Departments of Municipal Affairs and Public Works. The representatives start out condescending, since the Department of Telephones is relatively new and almost completely decentralized. She suppresses her initial hostile reaction against the arrogance of the capital, internalized from conversations with people like Anna, and instead uses their presumptions to lull them into thinking that they can tell her more than they normally would. At the same time, she plants the seed that an improved telephone system is particularly important, especially since rapid and reliable communication is necessary to coordinate projects from a centralized location, with offhand comments and suggestions. At the end of the day, she is content with the progress that she has made and is confident that she can play her desired role when she is back in Kralovna.

Buzzed from a potent mix of anticipation, success and a dash of alcohol, she returns home quite late to find Léon jotting something down in his notebook and the girls already in bed. With nothing pressing in the outside world, the need to concentrate on walking the line to get where she wants to go, with all its attendant concerns and anxieties, finally fades away. She contemplates Léon for a moment; a solid, steady presence. She almost lost that basic certainty in Kralovna, even when she recognized that it was this very nature that undoubtedly made it so difficult for him to write to her.

"You didn't write to me," she says softly as she slowly walks behind him and drapes her arms over his shoulders.

"Yeah, I'm sorry," is all that Léon can think to say. He pushes out a chair and gently pulls Lora around until she is sitting in front of him and they can look in each other's eyes. He keeps hold of her hand, maintaining the physical contact that they both acutely miss.

A moment of silence passes before Léon says, "I don't know why I find it so difficult to write to you." Then, with a smile: "But I will send you something." The unsaid 'when you are gone' hangs in the air of the kitchen.

Lora matches Léon's smile and pulls him up from the table. They make their way, with various pauses and detours to their bedroom, retreating from the kitchen, the room of discussion and planning, marked indelibly by efforts to put being reasonable and rational before passions and poetry. Léon's notebook rests on the table, forgotten for the night.

Chapter 14

Lora is gone once more. For Léon and the girls, the visit seemed like an interregnum from what their daily lives had become, as opposed to a return to normal or the beginning of a new chapter. Everyone's lives had been evolving at a different pace, and Lora's presence was not a significant enough event to bring the whole family into alignment. These days, Léon feels that the only alignment to be had for him comes whenever either Natalie or Eugenie drags him along to help them with whatever new whim takes their fancy. The situation has become marginally less stressful since he has learned to go along with it and just try to keep everyone grounded, but that is more than offset by the fact that he has to be involved at all. That in turn is outweighed by his desire to help his daughters through this learning process as unscathed as possible. He is not entirely sure when his motivation shifted from keeping up his end of the agreement with Lora and making sure that her sacrifice would not be in vain to simply wanting to support his kids. Lora's visit gave him a moment to be with the most important person in his life, but it also made clear that she had become far less important in his interactions with their daughters.

The stress of the day comes from Natalie's desire to read banned books written by other people. In a variety of ways, he is relieved with this new direction. He finds that she is an excessively harsh critic, which makes him self-conscious about certain passages in his own books with which he was never quite satisfied. Normally he tries to keep a certain distance from his work once it is out in the world, so as to limit the desire to obsessively rewrite parts of it. It would perhaps be different had he actually been making noticeable improvements to the texts, but after a while he found that beyond a certain point the changes depended on his mood at a given moment and that he would flip back and forth, never completely content. With Natalie reading and critiquing the work though, it is difficult for him to keep that distance.

Beyond that, his solution to this dilemma has its own set of issues. He repeats as much to his daughter as himself that he was a very different person when the book was written, so neither of them can view it as the work of who he is now. It would not be reasonable to take ownership of and modify the output of another writer. The major issue is that, while Natalie is largely motivated by the unadulterated curiosity to expend her literary horizons, a part of her is motivated by the desire to get to know her father better through this mutual interest. To say that it is essentially a different person who was writing years ago under-mines this connection. Even without saying it, however, she has picked up on the significant difference between the dense, opaque style of the books and the laconic, realist style of his journal articles. There is no literary evolution that connects the two styles, that shows how Léon grew as an author. It is in a way better that she moves on to other novelists so as to avoid the question entirely.

Léon feels that he should find a way to acquire the books himself, both because it should be easier for him and because he should be the one taking on that sort of risk. Unfortunately, he does not have an egotistical reason to keep a store of them someplace, as he does with his own novels, and tends to only keep up with contemporary works that reach him in the same manner as he distributes his journal. He savors the irony of being as much at a loss when one of his daughters wants help finding things in the underground literary world as he has been when one of them needs him to be a decent father in an ordinary sense.

Hervé predicted Natalie's evolution of course but, despite being more than willing to play a part in delivering the books to a member of the younger generation, he is not very knowl-edgeable on who may be producing and storing them these days.

He points out, reasonably enough, that with his ongoing, regularly scheduled coffee with the police regarding his tables and the general goings-on in the café, he tends to not actively seek out details of what goes on beyond his walls. This leaves Léon the option of asking people within the distribution network with whom he is in direct contact and letting the word spread. Just as with the journal, the spread of his question is necessarily lost in the ether; one can only wait and trust that the network functions.

It only takes a couple of days for an answer to get back to him. It comes through Hervé as Léon has fallen back into his habit of staying home in the evenings. He had just sent two cardboard beer mats with the logo of a beer brewed mainly for export and tourists to his wife. About twenty years ago, they had a bottle each at an upstanding establishment that seemed to feel that beer taps would detract from the ambiance. They decided to play tourist that day, including foreign accents and a perpetual sense of being lost. It was a good day that, unlike the more substantive successes of the period – finding success as a jurist and a novelist – has never been marred by subsequent events. Now, as is his habit, Léon is writing a feuilleton about the experience, minus the presence of Lora. Hervé joins him at the conifer table, the perfect table to feel like an outsider looking at people pass by through the window.

"I have a potential answer to your book dilemma, and I don't like it at all."

"Why is that?"

"Because it involves a regular at the Metro. I don't understand how someone involved in books could frequent that place, and I wouldn't trust them."

The Metro Café is the café where most of the painters and other visual artists tend to congregate, despite Hervé's efforts to attract them to his place and fulfill his original dream. After he accepted that his café's niche was on the literary side of the artistic spectrum, he became somewhat sensitive to those involved with the written word going elsewhere.

"Unless you have a better idea…" Léon replies.

"I am going with you."

"You are going to close your café to go to the Metro?"

"Never, the café will stay open. I have people that can cover for me; I can't be at the café all the time."

"I don't think that I have ever seen that."

"Then it will be a new experience for you. You can write an article on it."

"The thought had already crossed my mind, yes. I wonder if the cars across the street will follow us or stay with the café. Or if they will call in reinforcements."

Hervé manages to find someone to run the bar for the next evening. At dinner that evening, Léon explains the situation to the girls without giving specifics of how he got the information, the name of the café or anything about Hervé. Natalie speculates about who the individual could be, betting that it turns out to be someone who owns a bookstore that has a hidden section in the back for special clients.

Eugenie is too distracted by the success of the issue of the newspaper she put together. Using the model of Léon's journal, the focus was on daily student experiences. The articles avoided experiences that were too personal or controversial, since everything had to be approved by the faculty advisor, while keeping a sense of realism that the students could relate to. It helped that the Committee promotes a sort of formal realism that is quite similar. It was in any case far better than the fluff of the inaugural issue and the advisor suggested that she share the editorial duties with Albert, who had in the meantime returned to school, from then on. She is excited and anxious about the responsibility and makes her father promise to continue to help her. Léon, overjoyed that this puts her on an even footing with Albert – rather than her just following his lead – promises to give her whatever help she needs. As it happens, Albert has grander ambitions than running a school newspaper, so he leaves Eugenie with most of the work and, since his ideals are for substantive change and against the government's formal approach, all the credit.

The next evening, Léon and Hervé take a tram to the Metro. Hervé is in a reflective mood, thinking more than usual about his legacy. Léon can tell that he wants to talk about it but is not foolish enough to express his thoughts on the tram. Léon can nonetheless guess the question: now that he had experienced the benefits of giving his daughters a glimpse of what creative types of his generation had been producing before they were banned and was actively going further down this path, would he also make efforts to open this world to others of the same generation? Hervé would deflect the obvious response that it is only Léon's daughters who are pushing him to act and that he has a special obligation to them as their father by saying, first, that the situation has changed now that he has seen the positive results and, second, that he obviously feels an obligation to a larger group if he keeps publishing and distributing other people's articles through his journal. It was only reasonable to limit himself to the journal before he knew what else he could accomplish. Léon would respond with a cautious wait-and-see approach; when his daughters have left the nest and if they do not suffer any major repercussions from what they are presently doing, he might consider doing other things. However it is doubtful that anything he does will result in attracting many people to the Unity.

Léon repeats this last thought out loud: "Eventually perhaps, if things go well, but it probably won't have much of an impact on the café."

Hervé nods forlornly. Léon can only conclude that that is the response he usually receives when he broaches the subject with a regular.

Léon and Hervé get off the bus and walk the final block and a half to the Metro. It is in a mid-block art nouveau building, with graceful curves and detailing. If they are taken aback by a style that does not scream marginalization, the black cars across the street confirm that this is the right place. Entering the establishment, they find more of the same simple, elegant sinuosity. The only part that escapes the elegance is a stack of tables in a corner, evidently for a patio that probably hasn't been set up since the surveillance started. The café is full without seeming crowded. Everyone is low-key, though it is too early in the evening to predict if people get more boisterous, as they do at the Unity, as the evening wears on. Despite an uncomplicated elegance far more refined than what the Unity offers, the ordinary coffee-house tables give Hervé the excuse he needs to put on airs.

"What is the guy's name?" Léon asks, realizing that he has no idea who it is they are looking for.

"His name is Thomas. Don't worry about trying to find him though, I'll just ask Cesar."

"Cesar?"

"The owner."

At that moment, Léon notices a well-dressed man heading towards them. He supposes that they look conspicuous, standing in front of the door.

"Hervé!" Cesar calls as he reaches them, seemingly delighted to see his fellow café owner. After a quick kiss on the cheek he turns to Léon, waiting for Hervé to introduce his friend.

"Cesar, this is Léon; Léon, Cesar," Hervé says without enthusiasm.

"Any friend of Hervé's…" Cesar says warmly, shaking Léon's hand and nodding his head.

Léon wonders what he is in the middle of: "I didn't know that you knew each other."

"Oh, we are old friends, but we haven't seen each other in

many years. Not since I opened the Metro; it seems like a lifetime ago."

"We are looking for a fellow named Thomas," Hervé says, evidently uncomfortable discussing old times.

"You aren't going to try to snap him up for the Unity, are you?" Cesar asks, shaking his head and only half joking.

Hervé does not dignify the question with any attention at all.

"I would just like to talk to him," Léon responds, trying to put Cesar's focus on him.

"Ah. Performance art Thomas or bookish Thomas?"

"Likely bookish."

"He is third from the end," Cesar nods in the direction of a bench upholstered with amaranth velvet that runs along the entire wall.

Léon thanks Cesar and starts walking towards the bench. After a second, he realizes that Hervé is not following him, so he turns to see Cesar and Hervé retreating together to a short counter on the opposite site of the room. Léon shrugs and continues to the bench. The man Léon takes for Thomas is listening distractedly to a conversation on the border between lively and subdued, occasionally bringing a small glass of brandy to his lips without seeming to actually take a sip. Luckily, he is at the edge of a table, so Léon is able to come close before addressing him.

"I understand that you are Thomas?" Léon opens.

"It is not an especially unusual name."

"True enough. May I sit?"

"I don't see why not. My friends are having a rather feverish discussion, relatively speaking, on the significance of haloes in the fifteenth century. Perhaps you have some insight on the subject."

"I'm Léon, and I'm afraid that that is one of the shortcomings of my education," Léon says, sitting down on the bench beside Thomas, between tables.

"Then I suppose we will have to find a new subject, and a glass of something for you to ensure that the inevitable pauses in a conversation between people barely acquainted do not prove awkward." He signals a server, who brings another brandy. "I have found that it is best to not overextend the intelligence of the servers here by ordering something different."

Léon smiles: "Brandy suits me just fine."

"Brilliant. Now on to the subject. I suspect that you have something in mind."

"I do, as it so happens. Can I assume that one can speak freely here?"

"Freely enough, though certain artists tend to be shockingly prudish."

"So this café is frequented mainly by artists?"

"Are you trying to change the subject before it is even introduced?"

"I am just curious why you are here."

"Why don't we just assume that I like it here until we know each other better?"

"Okay, the subject then: I understand that you have access to books from the past twenty-odd years that are not as freely available as one might like."

"Ah. Why don't you tell me a bit more about yourself, Léon?"

"I suspect that you have from time to time read a modest journal that I put together. I'm afraid that there is little I am willing to say that goes beyond the journal's pages."

"I do know of this journal. Excepting the pieces by Lucien, who is as I understand it no longer in the position to contribute, it reads like an adolescent's diary; full of whiny self-importance."

Léon grins, thinking about how well the style went over for Eugenie. "That does indeed sum up my existence."

Thomas pauses to wet his lips. "Okay, books. What do you think I do?"

"Officially?"

"Besides pretending to drink brandy, listening to conversations that hold little interest for me, yes."

"I imagine that you are somewhere along the line from creating to selling books. You are an editor, publisher, printer or bookseller."

"I teach typing at a secretarial college."

"I never would have thought of it, but that makes sense too."

"If you are looking for perfection, you won't find it here."

"I would never presume."

"But you were thinking it; you were imagining a treasure trove of handsomely bound copies from the official runs."

"I suppose I was."

"Rather than a stack of A4s typed up by students learning to use a typewriter."

"That is how the journal is copied. I type all the copies myself."

"That explains a lot."

Léon feels that it is the opportune time to wet his lips with his brandy.

"Ha!" Thomas says. "I touched a nerve. Is this moment going to make it into your next, what do you call them, right, feuilleton?"

"Perhaps. In any case, a stack of A4s is perfectly fine. How do you distribute it?"

"The garbage at the college. I put everything together, you just have to pick it up before the waste collectors arrive."

"And for people under surveillance?"

"That is for you to figure out."

"Okay. Do you need a list?"

"You are not the first to ask for a 'variety'. You will have two novels a week for the next six months, in the trash every Thursday. And in return…"

"Yes?"

"Your journal is in high demand, no accounting for taste I

suppose. You will find a way to get a copy of your journal to me, here, as soon as you have typed the first copies." He pauses, looking at Léon's fingers, then grimaces. "Send me the copy that has the fewest errors."

"Hold off having the books typed for a week; I have to figure out how to make it work. And the journal too."

"For the journal, Cesar can help you out."

"Good to know. Thank you." Léon rises from his seat before Thomas stops him.

"The curiosity is killing me: I know that you wrote several of the classics – rocketman is a personal hero, by the way – and I can't imagine that you haven't read all the classics at one time or another. So, why do you want them now?"

"I am starting to feel out of touch with that time. On a whim, I reread one of my own books and I felt that a stranger had written it. It's funny; I hear a lot of talk about how the culture of my generation is not being passed on to the next one, since the Committee has realized that it is easier to control a population with no memory or heritage beyond what they decide to impose, but it isn't just the next generation. I feel like I am losing my own culture and while I kept my own books, it did not cross my mind at the time to do the same with all the books removed from the shelves at about the same time. Maybe once I've refamiliarized myself with them, my journal won't come off as adolescent whining."

"Don't be so sure; navel gazing seems to have been a prerequisite for getting published back then."

"I think that we have all become a bit cynical over the years." Léon finishes with that and walks to the front. Hervé notices and joins him there. Once they are in the street and some distance from the black cars, Léon recounts the pertinent details of his conversation. Hervé listens, nodding. When Léon is finished, Hervé points out that one of the Unity regulars, the poet who wrote most of the incomprehensible verse of the dinosaur/bird table, is a waste collector by day and would probably be fine with picking up the books. Regarding the journal, he thinks that that would be more difficult. The journal does make its way to a substantial number of clients of the Metro, just not directly. After some thought, he suggests that he and Cesar could possibly coordinate their visits to the state liquor wholesaler. He impresses on Léon that there are no guarantees and that Léon would have to do something for him in return. Léon accepts the condition so long as his best effort would be good enough. He can't guarantee anything either. In order to speak freely, if at a low voice, they walk back to the Unity, which leaves a half dozen blocks after they agree on the plan and its conditions and the two parting company for Hervé to imagine that his café had burned down in his absence. They part ways with two blocks to go. Even though Hervé can see that his café is still standing, he pays little attention to Léon's thank you and barely contains himself from running the rest of the way.

Chapter 15

Once more, Lora finds herself on the train; once more the emptiness of the uniform prairie stretches before her to the horizon. This time though, the fields are carpeted with the green of young wheat. Léon accompanied her to the station, only this time it wasn't the realization of a plan they had discussed well in advance. It was the continuation of the night before, staying together, feeling each other's warmth, as long as possible. There had been so many barriers between them when she arrived in the capital. She saw that her family had moved on without her. It was freeing of course; she can't remember a time when she had such independence to pursue her own projects, but it was also isolating. In a way, she felt more out of place in her own house than in the apartment in Kralovna. The barriers were an illusion though, built by unreasonable expectations that her family would not significantly change and yet that she would be able to become someone like Violet. With Léon last night, up until their long embrace before she got on the train, there were no expectations, just mutual understanding. Lora imagines that that is the sort of understanding that Arria had with her husband. Her sacrifices and his political indiscretions aside, there was a continuous thread of shared happiness.

As the train progresses along the perfectly straight line to Kralovna, Léon's touch cedes its place to his words regarding Maurice and the charter. Preoccupied with the meetings and Violet, she did not fully absorb the story of Maurice's past. Now that she knows that he was a famous classical pianist and has some time to reflect, some of the details of the trial come back to her. The official charges were that he was in possession of banned sheet music and that he played the music for more than one person. He had bought the music when it was legal to do so, but as it was transcribed by someone who emigrated some time later, the possession of the work became illegal after the fact. This is the same thing that happened to Léon's books and a significant portion of the cultural output from ten to thirty years ago. The motivation for the prohibition was a mix of removing works that did not conform to the Committee's worldview from the shelves, ensuring that everyone would be guilty of something, and reinforcing the monopoly of guilds and licensed artists.

Lora tries to think of the reason for him being arrested at that time in particular, but nothing comes to mind. Subversion was and continues to be a way of thinking though, so the trigger for the police is generally difficult to pin down and impossible to prove in court. At any rate, Maurice's dossier, like all such files, was several hundred pages long and contained enough about his life to pick the crime that would be the most useful and the easiest to prosecute. For artists, the prosecutors frequently choose transgressions linked to the profession, to make revoking the license or guild membership easier.

She remembers parts of the argument of the defense. They could not argue the possession of the sheet music, but that was in any case the lesser of the two charges. Regarding the performance, the lawyer argued first that, since the composer was not the same as the person who had transcribed it and subsequently emigrated, the music itself was not banned. Given that music that is played is fundamentally different than the notes on the page, Maurice's performance was legal. The lawyer went on to describe the music as a central piece in the national awakening, based on traditional peasant dances, and so was inalienable from the identity the government actively promoted. As such, it could not be against the law.

The other part that sticks out, now that she is thinking about it, is some difficulty they had with a couple of the witnesses. The prosecution called a couple of people present the evening in question to the stand and asked them while holding up the first leaf of the sheet music if Maurice had played the pieces. Added to the usual awkwardness of witnesses who find themselves in the unenviable position of denouncing their friends was the fact that, since the evening was just an informal get together at Maurice's house, there wasn't a printed program and Maurice had not announced what he was playing. Coupled with the fact that the witnesses could not read music and that it would have been rather inappropriate to have the music played in the courtroom, everyone was at a loss as to what to do. Lora ended up dismissing the witnesses and basing the decision on the police report and testimony.

The trial was of course only for form; everyone knew what the outcome would be before it started. Those who believed in the system were confident that these sorts of processes were necessary to maintain order. The Committee had to separate subversive elements from the general population so that life could continue predictably and safely. Those who didn't believe in the system felt that they had too much to lose in fighting it. Lora knew of a number of idealists who dreamed of a popular uprising, like what happened in other countries. They did not take into account that these uprisings were accompanied by significant poverty or some crisis that resulted in the population having little to nothing going for them. Here, life is not at all bad – at least materially – and the Committee does not care what happens privately so long as people maintain the appearance of following the rules in the presence of others. Most people seem to be able to accept this sort of existence.

It was of course a rude awakening for her and Léon when she realized exactly what was expected of her as a judge and, at about the same time, his books were banned and he was ousted from the guild. That was when they had their first serious kitchen table discussion. They decided to be what the idealists would call cowards; to work for the most part within the system. Léon needed to continue to write, that was clear from the beginning, but so long as his writing was not incendiary and she could keep her nose clean as a judge, they could live a relatively peaceful yet not untenably hypocritical life. Her becoming pregnant soon after cemented their commitment to this route.

Unfortunately, not all families survive the surveillance and harassment, let alone time in prison. She does not know what happened to Maurice after he left the courtroom, but it is not hard to guess. It is difficult to keep up the appearance of following the rules when one is around someone of interest to the police, and the police are not subtle in reminding people of that fact. The point is to make their target a pariah so that the disease of subversion does not spread. Maurice probably lost everyone close to him as well as the official sanction to express himself as a musician. She has seen it a thousand times in the faces of defendants and their friends and family, in court to testify against them. Léon enjoys pointing out from time to time that one is not free until one has a questionable record. He can talk to anyone without fear of repercussions because the police are already harassing him. So long as he is not committing a crime – talking to people, frequenting a café, etc. are not in and of themselves crimes – there is little more the police can do. It is a nice sentiment, but it doesn't hold when kids are in the picture. Lora wonders if Maurice has children, children that he can never see again without risking ruining their future.

The situation with Natalie and Eugenie puts the route into question though. Now that they are taking risks of their own volition, does she have the same obligation to limit her ambitions to working as a laborer in a yard? In the capital, when she first saw what was happening, her reaction was 'no'. It made her feel less guilty about her desire to take on what she sees as a more important and more interesting role. She wants the freedom Léon talks about without tarnishing her record. And it is not as if Léon is keeping to the original plan. She knows that it is not the same, that he has changed direction to try to limit the negative consequences of the girls' experimentation. She feels like every reason she comes up with to justify where she wants to go is a half-baked rationalization for a decision already made.

Lora takes a breath and looks around the car. It is half full of people from the capital; all of them trying to take up as little space as possible. She finds herself once more wishing that there was a Claude or an Anna sitting across from her, to distract her from her own thoughts. She never would have described the people from the capital as wanting to disappear into their seats before her time on the prairies. Now that she knows more, it doesn't strike her as much of a life, putting so much effort into not being noticed. And yet none of them, her included, would take the risk to stand out.

The charter, if it actually becomes a reality, would be an interesting experiment. As Léon described it, there would be no revolutionary or idealistic bluster; it would simply remind the Committee of its own obligations under the country's constitution. It would violate the unwritten rule that the Committee, along with the entire government apparatus, is infallible. This is the reason why everyone who is charged with a crime must be found guilty, since the police would not arrest an innocent person. Yet the message is reasonable; people should be able to expect to enjoy the basic freedoms that are guaranteed by law. Yet most of the population is like the people in this car. If the document is signed, it will be by the usual suspects; the artists and intellectuals who have already been blacklisted and erased from official discourse.

Léon spoke of a new wave of arrests among the underground musicians and writers that went counter to the balance tacitly agreed to between the community and the police. So long as the non-conformity was not overtly disruptive and the Committee had not taken a special interest, the police limited their operations to surveillance and harassment. That is how Léon has been able to produce and distribute his journal without significant problems. If that has changed, then the motivation for the charter is clear and the idea of popular support secondary. Since prison is the last tool in the police's arsenal and every one of these black-listed artists is already guilty of something, this creates exactly what is missing up until now; a situation where they have nothing to lose.

Lora pre-emptively chastises herself for coming up with another rationalization to become like Violet. The balance in the family between her and Léon relies on his activities being minor enough to be canceled out by her clean record and highly respected job. If the police have started to act more severely against similar work, it is only a matter of time before he is arrested. Since he knows about the charter and frequents people directly involved in it, there is also a good chance that he will run into problems even if the journal isn't specifically targeted. Now that there is no real distance between Léon's literary world and their family life, Natalie and Eugenie would not be able to escape without consequences. She doubts that they would ever end up in prison, but not being allowed to go to university would not be unthinkable. Suffice to say that a shift in the police's approach puts their original plan in question.

Lora consciously turns her thoughts away from vacuous rationalizations. The obvious solution that comes to her mind is to have the girls live with her in Kralovna. That would re-establish the distance between them and their father and limit the impact of the fallout from police overzealousness. She knows however that they would be very much against the idea, which brings her back to the impossible questions of what her role should be and how far she should go when her girls are determined to explore the world that has been closed to them until now. Beyond that, as much as she felt out of place at the house, it was heartwarming to see a real connection between Léon and his daughters.

Chapter 16

It is only the beginning and the flow of books from Thomas is overwhelming; mainly because a book a week is quite rapid when they can only be read in the evenings, but also because being typed on A4 paper makes them large and unwieldy, so Léon cannot simply put the book in his pocket when Natalie is finished reading at the end of the evening. His own books are in pocketbook format, so he was able to keep the one Natalie was in the middle of reading on him during the day. With this new format, he is obliged to keep more of the books in his locker at the library for longer periods of time. Since his locker is already rather full of his scribblings, he has to create some order and get rid of some of his papers. He enjoys the process, as chaotic messes leave him vaguely anxious. However, the police stationed across the street from the library notice this potential destruction of evidence and bring him and some of his papers in. The inspector gathers the pile Léon has just put in the garbage, all of which central has already combed through more than once, in a box. Léon is quite upbeat, since the feuilleton he has already started in his mind about sorting through old papers is going to be far more dramatic with police involvement. Happily, the police do not pay attention to the papers still in the locker, so do not notice the books.

"Would you like a cup of coffee?" the inspector asks pleasantly, once they have installed Léon in an agreeable enough little room. The table and chairs are a darkly stained pine that contrasts well with the white painted walls and ceiling.

"Please," Léon replies with a smile.

The inspector glances at his assistant, who is sitting off to the side with a pen and a pad of paper. She leaves the room to get the coffee.

"It is a lovely day, don't you think?"

"Mmm," Léon says noncommittally.

The assistant comes back with three cups of coffee, places the cups on the table and then settles in with her pen and paper.

"What is your opinion of…?"

"I refuse to testify."

The interrogation follows its typical path, with the inspector trying to suss out what and how Léon thinks – opinions are far more important than actions or other aspects of external reality – and Léon admitting nothing. Léon feels comforted by the back and forth, which is in a way easier to take than the shifting sands of the discussions he has with his daughters at the kitchen table. He is tempted to incorporate a line from Pliny – "I will tell you my opinion," I said, "If that is a matter to be brought before the court." – but there are far too many pitfalls in it.

After about half an hour, the inspector comes to the locker:

"What is your opinion of what is written here?" The inspector puts one of the sheets from the garbage on the table.

"I do not see anything written on the paper, so I am not sure what you are asking."

"The words, sentences, paragraphs on the paper; what is your opinion of them?"

"As the paper was found in the garbage, I imagine that it belongs there. As to the content, I refuse to testify."

"Why were you emptying out your locker?"

"My locker?"

"The locker you put your papers in."

"As much as one wishes to hold on to everything, catalogued for posterity of course, there is only so much room in a library locker. Once in a while, one is forced to cut down a bit."

"And how do you choose which papers to put in the garbage?"

"I am only speculating, but papers that everyone important has already read seem to be good candidates."

"I would like to wrap this up before lunch, Mr. Chaulieu, so just a couple more questions."

According to form, they had to take a break for lunch and the person being interrogated has the right to coupons for the cafeteria. The police cannot be seen as being anything but exemplary in the pursuit of their duties. This falls apart somewhat in the street, as Albert and Eugenie learned earlier, and is completely unimportant for cases off the books, but for official interrogations at the central station no one is purposefully mistreated.

"Please, continue," Léon says.

"What is your opinion of the P. L. Courier High School's new student newspaper?"

The question takes Léon by surprise; the locker incident is so closely linked to Natalie's situation that it did not even occur to him that they would also be interested in Eugenie. However, with Albert's involvement and their interest in him, he should have been able to predict this. His initial thought is to respond with "It seems to me that you would be further ahead posing that question to the students," but that might be taken as tacit consent to bring Eugenie in.

"I am not familiar with how student newspapers work so please correct me if I am wrong," Léon finally says, "but aren't all the articles approved by the faculty before anything is printed?"

"You are correct."

"Then, although I will not testify to the fact, I suspect that all student newspapers reflect a way of thinking that is in harmony with society and thus exemplary for society's younger members."

"Which is hard to believe, wouldn't you say, in the case of P. L. Courier when your daughter is the editor?"

"I cannot testify to the education my daughter receives at school, principally because I have no involvement in it. I would hope however that she is receiving the high level of instruction typical to state schools, an instruction that promotes a way of thinking that is in harmony with society. Would not a student newspaper be part of this instruction?"

"We have evidence, Mr. Chaulieu, that this particular newspaper was founded with intentions that are not in harmony with society. While the teachers involved with it have done an excellent job in ensuring that the end product reflects our society's values, it would be unfortunate to find out that Eugenie is working against those efforts."

The inspector pauses, giving Léon a chance to react and defend his daughter. Léon stays silent, knowing that the only way he can defend her is to betray his own involvement, which would just make things worse for her. The irony is that both Léon and Eugenie already censor their work, so using a common scare tactic such as this falls flat. Léon does not bother digging for a specific reason for the inspector's threat since it is undoubtedly no different than that which motivated the police to search the house after Lora left; a pre-emptive, opportunistic warning. Still, despite all that has happened since the search, he feels a hole in the pit of his stomach in hearing Eugenie's name spoken out loud by an interrogator, something that hasn't happened since just after she was born. It is another reminder of just how far they have come in such little time.

The expression on Léon's face while he takes a cup of coffee with an inspector is always a bit distant since his natural state is to be lost in thought. This is punctuated by the smile he regularly flashes, bordering on and occasionally slipping over into an overly intense grin. His thoughts normally concern how he can adapt the session into a feuilleton, but the expression does not change when they wander elsewhere. The interrogator, who is hoping to get a rise if not a defense out of Léon by the sudden change of direction of the interrogation and using Eugenie's name, is disappointed by the lack of visible reaction. He is not astonished by it – he is perfectly aware that Léon is not exactly a novice – but that does not stop him from hoping for something more.

After an instant, the inspector thanks Léon for his time and cooperation, and accompanies him to the main entrance. Léon thinks that he made a mistake by not prolonging the session so that they would provide him lunch and he could see if anyone he knew showed up at the cafeteria. That thought evaporates with the summer heat intensified by the exposed boulevard and uniform white buildings of the government complex. His usual destination after an interrogation that does not take all day is the Unity, in order to give some form to the incipient feuilleton in his head.

When he arrives at the café, he is at a complete loss as to where to sit. His mind is in turmoil from the intrusion of his family into yet another space that had been separate for so long. The purely literary world has shrunk once more, and he feels increasingly constrained. What will happen when there is no separation at all? Will he stop writing? He can't stop writing but that means he will inevitably betray his family. Hervé, after contemplating the unmoving figure in the doorway, comes over to lead Léon to the symmetry table, a fairly discreet table close enough to the counter so that he can easily keep an eye on him.

"Do you want to talk about it?" Hervé asks.

Léon shakes his head and pulls out his notebook without immediately opening it.

"If you would like," Hervé adds, changing the subject, "we can store some of the books in the stack of paper by the typewriter at the fungus table for a while."

Léon nods and manages to say, "That is a good idea."

Hervé retreats to prepare a pot of lemon tea, which he silently brings to the table. When it is adequately over-steeped, Léon pours a cup and inhales the aroma, eyes closed. He finally opens his notebook and starts in on his original idea; the difficult task of culling old papers and the suspicion the activity raises amongst those observing him. The emotions aroused by his narrowing literary world finish by fueling the work at hand, which takes the form of a requiem for inferior work. His concentration leads him into early evening, until he feels Hervé's hand on his shoulder and a friendly suggestion that it was perhaps time to head home to make dinner. Léon responds with another nod, finishes his sentence and leaves the café without a word.

Léon's thoughts shift back to his family once he is out in the street. His passion exhausted by the afternoon's writing, his reflection is calm and peaceful. He thinks that he might have underestimated how far the police have gone in regards to Eugenie; perhaps she has already had a cup of coffee with an inspector or was involved in trying to sneak some non-conformist ideas past the faculty sponsor. In any case, the situation will become clearer when he arrives home, so he might as well take the opportunity to enjoy his ignorance.

When he enters the house, he realizes that he did not have a chance to take one of Thomas's books from the locker for Natalie to read. He passes by the living room, where she is reading a novel of antiquated values that she has read at least once before. In order to hold to their agreement, he knows that he will have to at least summarize what had happened that morning, but for the moment he just apologizes for not having the opportunity to bring another book home.

He then passes into the kitchen, where Eugenie looks as angry and upset as she was when she waved around a copy of his journal and blamed him for ruining her life. Natalie, who is not profoundly interested in what she is reading, follows him and sits down at the table. Food does not seem to be a priority for the moment, so after a brief hesitation between the counter and the table, Léon joins his daughters at the table.

"What's on your mind?" Léon asks Eugenie.

"They shut the newspaper down," she exclaims irately.

"Who is 'they'?"

"The school," Natalie responds helpfully.

"Right," Léon says, "but who specifically?"

"The faculty sponsor and the principal," Eugenie says, her voice sliding into bitterness. "The two people who supported it from the beginning. They were so supportive and then bam! They say that it can't continue."

"There has to be more to it than that."

"I pushed them, forced them to tell me the truth, and you know what? They claim to be trying to protect me. By lying to me, by taking away what I – what we – worked so hard on. Sound familiar?"

"I suppose it does," Léon responds self-consciously.

"Do you think that trying to keep me in a box really protects me?"

"Well, yes, after a certain fashion, but not in a good way."

"Albert is not even involved any more, we did so much to make sure that nothing unacceptable was included, we did so much to make sure that it wasn't superficial garbage, what right did they have to take all that away?"

"I can sympathize. The bitterness and frustration I felt when they banned my books was indescribable."

"The worst part is that it isn't just me they are hurting. Other kids, even some who made my life hell, have come to me to talk about their lives because the articles spoke to them. That school is like a prison; everyone is too scared to say what they think. And the teachers smother the only glimmer of hope. I was helping people." The last sentence is whispered with tears in her eyes.

In a moment that seems like a mirror image of the day the police took Natalie's books away, Natalie takes her sister's hand. Everyone sits in silence; there is nothing to say. Léon decides that recounting his morning's adventure can wait until another day.

Chapter 17

Lora enters the meeting room a couple of minutes after Phillip, using the excuse of having to go to the washroom. He saves her a place at the table, but she chooses to sit along the wall instead. This is the first formal meeting she has attended since her visit to the capital, but she has used her debriefing with Phillip, along with various opportunities in passing, to get her suggestions across in a way that has made it seem like he had arrived at the conclusions himself, but that her questions and advice has been invaluable to help him put all the pieces together. Everything has been working just about as well as she could have hoped.

She also has an unrelated reason to be optimistic; she received two beer mats in the mail from Léon that she recognized straight away. While they say nothing about how the family was presently doing – a hope that she has in any case decided is unrealistic – they serve as a reminder of the happiness that the two of them have shared for so long. And that is enough for now.

The meeting is being held in the same room as the one with the railroad people, in the office annex of the station. Apparently, all the departments and agencies from the capital prefer it, as they can come and go without actually being in Kralovna proper. The railroad enthusiastically supports the use of their space, as it reinforces the idea that a railroad station is a hub for everything and facilitates informal side meetings elsewhere in the office area. It also suits the Department of Telephones because it is easier to stretch the truth about their operations and materials needs when their partners and suppliers can't be bothered to look at their facilities. For these reasons, this tendency is a cornerstone of Lora's project and the main seed she planted in the capital; improving the telephone network is central for other depart-ments as a means for them to manage their assets outside the capital without leaving town.

Today's meeting is with representatives from the Department of Municipal Affairs.

"Thank you all for coming out to Kralovna to meet with us," Phillip begins. "Perhaps we can start with a round of introductions."

Historically, Municipal Affairs would have insisted that any meeting would have to be held in their offices in the capital. With the plan that they presented earlier to take control of utilities that needed significant capital investment from municipalities across the country though, they decided that a token effort to show that they are active outside the capital would be prudent.

The agenda starts with a short summary of the progress Municipal Affairs has made on their plan in order to put it front and center in the conversation. The head of the delegation gives a couple of words thanking the Department of Telephones for setting up the meeting and taking an interest in municipalities before passing off the responsibility of going over the state of the plan's implementation. The second official explains that they have an omnibus agreement in principle to take over all local utilities with approximately ninety percent of all smaller municipalities, with a population between 10,000 and 50,000, in return for paying off current debt and funding critical improvements. Once field inspectors have finished their assessments and the numbers are crunched, the formal agreements can be signed. The remaining smaller municipalities, as well as the larger ones, will be approached individually at a later date.

"The agreements in principle are, I take it, open until the inspectors have finished their assessments?" Phillip asks.

"Yes, since they ultimately need to include asset lists. The systems themselves are relatively simple as it turns out; it is the maintenance yards and equipment that has proven more difficult, especially in smaller towns where everything is shared between utilities and other services."

It is generally easier to join existing agreements, so long as they are not finalized and are recent enough so that the people who were involved at the beginning are still present.

"Are you planning to keep the current maintenance staff as it is?"

"Only where road conditions make it impractical to combine operations."

"What sort of area will the operations centers cover?"

"Optimally, maintenance crews should be able to be on-site within three hours. The distance depends on the roads, though hopefully Public Works will bring the whole network up to a decent standard before too long."

"How much independence will they have?"

"As minimal as possible. We would like to coordinate all operations, except for emergencies, centrally."

These are exactly the responses that Lora and Phillip were expecting.

"I imagine then that telephones are part of your strategy."

"They would be very helpful for linking the central office to the operations centers, and the operations centers to locals."

The departments in the capital still view the telephone as a new technology that can support activities but is not central to them. Lora suggested in the capital that it should be thought of as rather more fundamental. While the Municipal Affairs representative underplays its importance with 'very helpful' it is clear from the department's aspirations that they are considering it as necessary. The only way to achieve three hours between when an incident is reported and a response from a center in another town, particularly on the prairies where the towns are further apart, is if the center can get an immediate, accurate and detailed incident report. At this point in time, that is only possible with the telephone. If Municipal Affairs is open about the response time in this meeting, that means that they have already talked about it, and set expectations, in the capital. Which is to say that they need the telephone system to work for them.

Phillip then briefly lays out the recent progress of the Department of Telephones, with a particular focus on the expansion of, and upgrades to, long distance lines. Once he has adequately shown that his department has been very active in the last several years and is close to being in the position to meet Municipal Affairs' needs, he switches gears to discuss those needs and associated difficulties.

"It is very forward thinking of you to consider telephones as a means to maintain the links between your offices. I am sure that we can help you meet your goals. At the same time, we share similar challenges in providing a high level of service across the country. While we regulate all telephone infrastructure, a significant number of municipalities control their own exchanges. This worked reasonably well at the beginning, but they have not had the resources to upgrade their equipment in a timely fashion. When external funding is provided and despite the regulations in place, the upgrades tend to be disorganized and inefficient. Since you are in the process of overcoming these types of challenges, perhaps there are opportunities to coordinate our efforts."

The people from Municipal Affairs are happy to give advice but are reluctant to involve the Department of Telephones in the agreement already underway. They are understandably concerned that the involvement of a new party could put a spanner in the works, resulting in everything falling apart. Phillip, of course, lets them bring up and then dismiss the possibility. It is only when he brings up timelines, and the fact that his department would be going slowly, feeling its way, to make certain that everything is done correctly – which can be translated as having neither the manpower nor the expertise to independently conclude such extensive agreements in a timely fashion – that adding them is reconsidered. Municipal Affairs is on a relatively aggressive timeline and, since the whole plan depends on a reliable telephone network, they need Telephones to follow a similar schedule.

In the afternoon, Lora is back in the yard with Anna and Maurice, unloading crossbars. She is elated at the understanding the departments arrived at that morning and her role in it. It was the first of her behind the scenes efforts that has come to fruition and she doesn't see a major obstacle for other efforts to result in the same sort of success in the future. Her efforts in the capital were, however, quite limited, so the next step is to suggest to Phillip that he would be well served to send her as an observer to other meetings, planning sessions and whatever else might come along. This step, like so many others, is directly inspired by how she views Violet, who moves around a great deal and seems to be involved in all sorts of deals. Lora pauses to wonder why Violet was not at this morning's meeting, but quickly explains it away; even Violet cannot be everywhere at once.

Lora is also happy to still spend a great deal of time in the yard, particularly now that her body has adapted to the work and her mind is more at ease with the lack of information regarding her family. The original idea of moving from a precarious situation in the capital to one that is above reproach here is perhaps even more important now that she is taking more risks. Beyond that, it is pleasant to not have to concern herself with motivations, influence, deals, etc. all the time. It does not make sense to replace the moral fatigue associated with being a judge or with anxiety about her family with something just as draining.

Although she is still far from feeling free enough to take Maurice up on his offer to give her piano lessons, after the success of that morning, coupled with her new knowledge of who he is – or was – she does not consider putting some effort into talking to him as unreasonable. She approaches him when Anna is on one of the cars unlatching the final strap.

"Why did you stop playing piano?" Lora asks, going directly to what she suspects is the heart of the matter.

"Are you really asking me that?" he responds, his voice

colored by resentment.

"You know the system pretty well; you know that the crimes you were charged with were chosen out of convenience."

"I still went to prison for them. How can I play without feeling that connection and everything I lost? Besides, why would I give the authorities more excuses to lock me up?"

"I don't know," Lora says, thinking of Léon, "I suppose that I have always assumed that creative, passionate people are willing to take those sorts of risks and can't really stop doing something so central to who they are without losing themselves."

Maurice just shrugs before changing his mind and responding: "But I wasn't even really playing, I was having a laugh with some friends over the government's bizarre reinterpretation of our so-called traditional, peasant culture. Do you think that every time a musician touches an instrument, there is some sort of transcendental creative experience? Do you think that, whatever the real motivations of the authorities happened to be, I went to prison for my art?"

He shakes his head and walks away, leaving the question of how he could just stop playing unanswered. Lora considers following him to ask why he had offered to teach her piano, but, noticing that Anna has been watching them from the car, decides that another time would be better. Anna lets the strap fall noisily to the ground, undoubtedly expressing her annoyance at being left out of the conversation. Lora pushes a crane to her and she attaches two crossbars before sending it back. She then does the same for the crane that Maurice approached at the same time. Lora and Maurice use the two tracks on either side of the stack that they are adding to today to move the crossbars without interfering or interacting with each other. They align the loads and carefully drop them on the stack and then return to Anna.

Lora resolves to consider the distrustful and not particularly friendly interaction with Maurice as a good thing. First of all, they actually spoke and she did learn something new about him and the circumstances leading up to his trial. Moreover, it put a check on her elation from the morning. Yes, the meeting was a success, but she has a long way to go to achieve the independence and trust that Violet seems to enjoy. Maurice's distrust also reminds her that there is a chance that she will never completely escape her previous occupation, especially since every judgment she made and opinion she expressed in the course of her duties are officially her own.

Chapter 18

The respect that Eugenie inspired with the newspaper ends up leaving a lasting impression on her schoolmates, which gives her some consolation for it being shut down. The cowardliness that she sees in what the teachers did, added to Albert's general absence, a result of his pursuit of other projects rather than any police action, and lack of concrete results, also gives her an appreciation of Léon's moderate approach. Both Léon and Eugenie know that she will feel the need to do more soon enough, but are for the moment content to let things lie. Letting things lie is however relative as she has decided that his cooking, which he would be the first to admit is quite limited, is inadequate and has expanded her role from helping him in the kitchen to taking the lead more often than not. Léon shares this with Lora by collecting the empty packages for new products, including notes on ingredients without packaging, and sending them to his wife under the heading 'Adventures in Food'. Léon imagines that one day, if he can find some money, he will buy a camera and send her pictures of the prepared food, among other things.

As for Natalie, most of the kinks have been worked out in the process to provide her with copies of the banned books. Léon and Hervé hedge their bets by storing most of the novels in the locker at the library and some in the stack of paper by the fungus table at the Unity. The police did come by the library once to confiscate all the papers in the locker, but it is too early to know if those books are lost. Normally the papers – or at least most of them – reappear after a couple of weeks, though he expects that he will be brought in for a cup of coffee at the very least if central notices the books. Either way, it will only be him who suffers the consequences, which is exactly how the process is set up to work.

Natalie has also decided that she likes picking up other people's dirty laundry. One day, she brought up the novel she was reading when the police searched the house, with the passive and pious daughter who had irritated her so much. She said that the author had a habit of describing everything – facial expressions, scenery, conflict, etc. – as poetry. She had taken it as an excessively artistic and idealized way of seeing the world, since poetry for her represented a sort of rarified beauty. Crisscrossing the city, entering houses and businesses by side entrances off alleys, she has come to appreciate a non-idealized, non-rarified sort of poetry. This realization has led her to the conclusion that her ignorance of the world may be hindering her appreciation of books. Her train of thought went much further, all the way to the doubt that she could really understand anything she read, but she pulled back to just keeping her job and profiting from it by becoming more familiar with daily life in the city.

Suffice to say, Léon thinks as he heads to the Unity, everything is going reasonably well. He stops short a couple of blocks away when he notices a truck in front of the café. A handful of laborers are loading the tables into it while several inspectors look on. Léon sighs; he recognizes that the confiscation of the tables is a regular, inevitable event, similar to the seasons, but that does not make it any less inconvenient and frustrating for everyone involved. At the very least, he wish there was some warning so that Hervé could rent some replacements and arrange for someone to manage the café while he is having coffee with a pair of inspectors in a warehouse on the other side of town. It would also be nice if Léon was able to take the typewriter and some paper so that he could get some work done elsewhere. On a certain level, the confiscation comforts him as it reinforces his notion of 'reasonably well'. With a couple of books stashed in the pile of paper though, it is hard to know how the interrogation will end this time.

Léon is not unduly concerned though, since he knows that the Committee prefers order and the police dislike expending significant effort to keep tabs on blacklisted artists. They know that if

Hervé is arrested and the Unity shut down, the regulars will scatter, which will make the job of maintaining order that much more difficult. This also happens to be one of the motivations for the police to tolerate Léon's journal, since it is a known quantity that is fairly low on the scale of subversion. If they shut down the journal, writers may be driven to more radical publications. It is unfortunate that the teachers at Eugenie's school and whoever has been behind the string of recent arrests are not so pragmatic.

In the past, he has used these days as an impromptu holiday. Today though, he is more motivated by the idea of refocusing his writing. The crisis the other day after hearing Eugenie's name uttered by an inspector was unhealthy, as is his inability to write to Lora and the complete break between before and after he was blacklisted. The pages read here and there of the books acquired for Natalie and the articles he helped Eugenie edit have somewhat broadened his perspective. Reading is far from writing though; his attempt to use Pliny's style to write to Lora was a failure, for instance. That just means that he should try something else, such as wandering around the city to get a sense of the flawed, common poetry that Natalie talks about.

At the end of the day, Léon is no better off. He saw poetry in abundance, but only in the context of a daily experience of a blacklisted writer who is trying to find inspiration in the small space between prison and family. Still, he continues to be of the opinion that life is going in a satisfactory direction and that he will find other subjects and styles that interest him in due course. He settles in to making dinner with Eugenie, who wants to try something new from a cookbook a classmate had lent her. They are just about finished when Natalie arrives from her pick-ups, more agitated than usual. Natalie is frequently excited when she gets home, impatient to describe whatever struck her the most, and Eugenie and Léon are preoccupied with preparing dinner, so they don't notice that she is animated by something else.

"Unity Café is empty, Hervé and the tables are gone," she

exclaims.

Eugenie's head shoots up and she looks at her father. She has never been to the café, but has heard enough about it in the last short while to realize how important it is to Léon. The possibility that something else significant to the family had been shut down hits her hard.

"It happens," Léon states calmly, continuing to stir the pot in front of him.

"It happens? It's normal?" Natalie asks, her excitement fading to disappointment at the subdued reaction to the big news.

Eugenie's attention does not shift from her father, the final ingredients to be added to the pot forgotten on the cutting board.

Léon glances up, wondering why Eugenie hasn't added the ingredients, and realizes that he needs to explain the situation.

"Yeah, it happens every year or so," he says, taking the board and dumping it. "In a week or less, it will reopen. It is just to remind Hervé and the regulars that the police can come in at any time, and so to not do anything foolish."

"The same reason they searched the house," Eugenie says quietly, mostly to herself.

"Yes, it is a fairly ordinary tactic."

"It also gives the people in the cars across the street some time off," Natalie suggests.

"The cars have been there quite some time," Léon says. "Why don't we have dinner?"

"Great! I'm starving."

Eugenie distractedly helps her father bring the food to the table.

"Hervé does not have a plan for keeping the café open in the meantime?" she asks.

"No. The police don't give much warning, so it is hard to organize things," Léon replies.

"He needs a partner."

"He has some difficulty in trusting other people with his café.

He was on edge when he had to leave it for a couple of hours to set up getting the books for Natalie. I can't imagine what a week would do to him."

"He helped with the books?" Natalie asks. "I didn't know that; that is awfully nice of him."

"He has a soft spot for younger people; he thinks that it is very important for the culture of his and my generation – and generations further back for that matter – to be passed on and not forgotten."

"You don't think that that is important?" Eugenie asks, detecting the note that creeps into her father's voice when he thinks an idea is too idealistic.

"I do, but as we all know, it is difficult to put the idea into practice when being in possession of a good portion of that culture is illegal. We have been able to make it work to a certain extent as a family, knowing the risks and accepting a great number of constraints. At a larger scale though…" Léon shakes his head.

"If it was at a larger scale though, the government wouldn't be able to stop it."

"Perhaps. I think you will find that most people are like the teachers at your school though, that they are not willing to take the risk even if they support the idea. The other hurdle is the need to produce thousands of copies in a short period of time; the sort of equipment needed to do that is locked down pretty tight."

Natalie, who is always hungry after working, checks out of the conversation to focus on the food. "This is really good," she says to her sister, not bothering to swallow before expressing her opinion.

"Thanks," Eugenie replies brightly. She takes a bite before turning her attention back to the dilemma her father has posed. "How do we get around that?" she asks Léon.

"My take is that the problem doesn't matter too much, but

that means that we can't set having popular support for what we do as a major goal." Léon is tempted to use his journal as an example, since it would still be just an idea had he waited for buy-in from other creative types, let alone a majority of the general population. He is concerned though by the wheels turning in Eugenie's mind; it is clear that the cooking is just a stopgap and that she has started to look for a way to put into practice Hervé's ideals one way or another. While he will try to be supportive of any project within reason that she comes up with herself, he doesn't want her to found an underground newspaper at her school just because he mentions the journal in this context. Of course, his preference would be that she focuses on the cooking regardless and that he never hears her name spoken by an inspector again.

"I suppose that we have to start somewhere."

"Haven't we already started – and accomplished – a lot already?"

"I guess so, given where we started anyway, but there is so much more we can do." Eugenie reads the hint of worry on her father's face: "That doesn't mean that we have to be stupid about it though. I just think that it is not right to do nothing."

"Also," Natalie adds, slowing her fork now that she is starting to feel sated and responding to an earlier point in the conversation, "we shouldn't fixate on books and journals and the like. There are so many other things out there in the world."

Chapter 19

Phillip waves at Lora to join him in the war room as she passes through the administration building. He seems unhappy, which Lora chooses to view as a signal that another opportunity is around the corner. If everything at the department was going perfectly smoothly, after all, there would be little of substance she could do to improve her situation. And her experience of late has only confirmed her initial supposition that substance is king on the prairies.

"First," Phillip says once Lora is installed at the table, "I want to thank you for the great advice you have given regarding the interests of other departments. When I first asked you to attend an external meeting, I was hoping that you would be able to provide these sorts of insights. Honestly, your contributions have gone well beyond my expectations."

This opening gives Lora an uneasy feeling; Phillip generally comes straight to the point. On the other hand, perhaps he is just getting an accurate sense of what she can offer.

"I am always happy to help out where I can," Lora says modestly.

"It is because of this assistance I suppose that I am not really surprised that the department received an order from the Committee regarding you."

The uneasiness turns to dread.

Phillip continues: "The Committee doesn't generally send us orders – they prefer to be very hands-off – so when they do, we generally take them seriously. The last thing that we want is to give them an excuse to become more involved in how we operate."

"What does it say?"

"It demands politely that you be moved from the yard into the field." Phillip hands the letter to Lora.

"No explanation, but that is typical," Phillip says while Lora reads the memo multiple times. "There is no use in speculating as to the reason, but you know that better than I. I hope that you didn't do anything risky in the capital just to help out the department."

Lora shakes her head: "I asked some representatives questions and gave certain people a better understanding of how the telephone system works, nothing more." Her mind races from Maurice asking Violet to intervene so that he would not have to work with the judge that sent him to prison to the government punishing her family for being in possession of banned books or sneaking a subversive article into a school newspaper. She knows that Phillip is right; she is perfectly aware that the Committee acts for obscure, incomprehensible reasons.

"What will I be doing in the field?" Lora asks quietly after a moment of silence.

"I am setting you up as an inspector. Go to the store in the exchange building for your field equipment. Tomorrow, you'll head out on the train to Los. One of our better inspectors will meet up with you at the station and show you the ropes.

"You know, I am unhappy to lose you here; I meant what I said about you being very valuable. That said, being an inspector is more varied work than being in the yard. You will not have the city amenities and be further from your family, but I think that you will appreciate the experience. Do you still have the train pass?"

She nods, having never even thought of giving it back after her trip to the capital.

"Good luck then." Phillip turns to focus his attention on other correspondence.

Lora leaves the letter on the table and walks out. In the hallway, she can't stop being angry at herself for taking the order so passively, despite understanding that kicking up a fuss would not have changed anything. She was just getting used to the idea that she could actively control her destiny in a far more significant way than choosing to leave the judiciary before the Committee decided to put her on trial. Maybe this wouldn't be happening had she kept her head down in the yard, maybe the Committee would take an interest in her no matter how much distance she put between herself and the capital; she will likely never know. She realizes that she is standing in the middle of the hallway and decides that she has nothing better to do than to visit the store.

As the store is run by the department, she expects that finding her gear will be a simple, practical experience. Instead, it is like finding herself back in the capital. The space is stuffed with barely organized equipment, very little of which is actually useful. After finding the clerk in the chaos, she asks him, "Is there a standard kit for field inspectors?"

"What sort of work do field inspectors do?" the clerk asks in turn.

Although she has little confidence that an explanation will be helpful, Lora explains as best as she is able, given her lack of experience.

"You should take some rubber boots and a headlamp or two. We have boxes and boxes of them. You'll probably even find something in your size."

Lora considers guessing what she will require and wading into the disorder before changing her mind and heading to the yard to ask Anna for her advice. She was hoping to avoid this, not wanting to have to deal with Anna's questions and Maurice's satisfaction to see her leaving. She figures that being in the field without the right equipment would be far worse though, so she will just have to get through it. She finds her two former workmates lounging on their preferred hello girls and tells them simply and directly that she is leaving the yard and could use Anna's help to choose the gear.

"This is so exciting!" Anna says, almost shouting. She jumps off her exchange and continues in a more moderate voice: "I mean, it might be hard for you, not being used to spending so much time in the countryside. We will miss you, too. But you will finally be able to see what we talked about, meet the farmers who have joined together to put up their own lines. That is where things actually get done."

"Do you miss being out there?"

"Sometimes, but that's not important. Let's see if we can't find what you need."

Maurice tries to embrace Anna's enthusiasm, but for him it is more of a hope than a belief that Lora will be better off on the open prairie. He wonders, since it is not typical for the government to control the minor details of people's lives out here, if she is leaving of her own volition, and how much of a role the discomfort of working around someone she had a part in sending to prison might have to do with it. He doesn't want to be a reason for anyone to choose a life that might make them miserable, but he can't bring himself to leave the trial behind him. She may not have been in control of how things went, but she willingly played her role, despite knowing how unjust it was and how much it was hurting people. Still, he hopes that she finds contentment with her new position. He follows Anna and Lora to the store just in case additional hands are needed.

"You understand that I have never been an inspector, myself," Anna says, taking in the incomprehensible jumble of goods in the store. "However, quite a number of inspectors came to take a gander at my loop back in the day. There are three things they looked at: the telephones, the line and the poles. You might also be testing repeaters that boost the signal on the line, which I didn't have to worry about since they were always on the department's side. You don't need anything special for the telephones as everyone uses standard models. The poles are simple, since you can recognize a seasoned, winter cut cedar pole in good shape from the work in the yard. You will just need a hammer to make sure there is no interior rot. The line could be more complicated; you might have to climb up to get to it. A standard lineman's kit should get you up to the top safely and a handful of meters, detectors and testers will give you all the information you need to make a call. I am assuming of course that they are setting you up with another inspector to teach you how to use everything and to not electrocute yourself or fall off a pole. Having the equipment means nothing if you don't know how to use it."

Lora just nods, feeling almost as lost as when she started in the yard. On top of that, she has a certain trepidation that the inspector who will be mentoring her will not be as engaged nor as helpful as Anna. The thought is fleeting though, as Anna directs her to start at one end of the store to look for large hooks and small electronic devices with displays showing a needle over range. Anna has Maurice start at the other end and she begins in the middle. Nobody pays any attention to the clerk, who in turn pretends that he is alone in his alcove of boxes.

It takes the rest of the morning, but the three of them manage to find what they are looking for. Lora and Maurice are surprised at the success, knowing that useless goods are more often than not shipped in place of needed equipment, rather than in addition to it. Perhaps there is a bit of the department in the store after all. Being cooped up in such a small space for several hours puts a damper on everyone's mood. Anna in particular is subdued in their triumph. After noticing the time, they head to the cafeteria together a final time. Maurice puts the testing equipment in the lineman's kit bag and follows Anna and Lora with the bag on his shoulder, at the same distance behind them as when they went from the yard to the store.

On the way to the cafeteria, Anna stops at an office to borrow a sheet of paper and a pencil. Once the three have gotten their food and made their way to a table, she jots down the coordinates of her family farm as well the names of people she has worked with over the years who are currently in the field. By the time she is done writing her energy has regained its pre-store level, buoyed by an endless stream of cherished memories.

"If you pass by the farm or run into anyone on this list," she instructs Lora, "tell them you know me. Even if you don't they will be happy to give you a hand whenever you might need it, but it always helps to let them know that you are already part of the community."

Lora does not have the impression that she is part of a community. Still, it can't hurt to have connections when there will be so few people around. She thinks back to Claude's story about the crippling loneliness of the early homesteaders and her own fears of further isolation and takes the list as if it is a talisman. The idea that she might not be able to trust them, an idea that had become second nature to her after a life spent in the capital, does not cross her mind.

Ironically, the belief she had that the Committee would leave her in peace in Kralovna, which was more or less the case in the capital, turned out to be unfounded. She can't have influence over anything without living in a city where at least some decisions are made and being close to a decision-maker like Phillip. On the other hand, the influence of the Committee should be all but nonexistent where she is going. She will be able to do whatever she wants, without the opportunity to do much of anything. The only realistic option is to fill the role the Committee has set out for her.

"I am going to be keeping the apartment in town," she says to Maurice. "If I drop off a set of keys before I leave, will you look in from time to time and pick up the mail?"

"Of course," Maurice responds with a slight smile, the first that Lora had seen. It reminds her somewhat of Léon.

Chapter 20

Léon's plan for the kitchen table has worked, though its success leaves him ambivalent. The idea was to discuss ideas, issues and whatever else as a family, just as he and Lora had done as a couple, so that nobody would act impulsively and leave everyone else to deal with the consequences. At the same time, there is so much that he would rather not know, since the most he can do is try to reason with his daughters. If one of them is going to run head first into a brick wall regardless of what he says, he would rather learn about it after the fact so he doesn't have to suffer from the anticipation and is not dragged into it in any way.

Hervé and the tables have yet to reappear at the café, which, despite less than a week having passed, feeds Eugenie's desire to do something in line with his ideals. Despite Léon's warning to not go by the Unity so often, Natalie takes a look on a daily basis and announces that it is still empty every day at dinner, which, to Léon's way of thinking, just makes things worse. She promises to be careful, to not go too close; she points out that the black cars are no longer across the street; none of this makes him feel any less uneasy. The situation comes to a head when Eugenie asks Natalie and Léon to sit back down one evening after the dinner dishes have been put away.

"We should do something for Hervé," Eugenie states matter-of-factly.

"Such as?" Léon responds, trying to recall his objections from the last time this subject was broached.

"That's what I want us to figure out. The day the police came to the café, we discussed the senselessness of doing anything beyond the family, but not long ago you thought that it was impossible to include me and Natalie in projects that cross this stupid, arbitrary line the government has imposed. And, in one way or another, we have all already moved beyond the family;

Natalie has moved beyond reading your books, I started something at school and your journal is read by all sorts of people. Even if he is not at this table, Hervé has helped both you and Natalie get through some tough situations. We have to recognize that we are part of something bigger and that we don't get to just brush aside other people's aspirations. Hervé may not be here, but that does not mean that he is not one of us."

"Maybe we can convince him to leave his café open," Léon suggests.

"Is that what he really wants?"

"No, it would take a lot of convincing."

"What does he want?"

"Well, he is a bit of a romantic. The Unity started out as a re-creation of some mythical, half-forgotten café frequented by poets and writers that posterity forgot even before the Committee started its banning spree. That evolved into a dream to relive the role of proprietor of a café from a scene in a film. He imagined a very different result when he suggested to his regulars to make his tables more interesting. After that he came into his own; instead of trying to copy another café, he started hoping that his café would be valued and remembered as an original. For that to happen though, your generation has to appreciate it. The problem is that almost nobody of your generation even knows that it exists.

"From there, it was a short step to pushing for all sorts of bits of culture to make it past the generational divide. Beyond suggesting to his regulars to invite younger people to the café, bugging me to get my journal into younger hands and helping us with acquiring books for Natalie though, he hasn't been very active in realizing this dream."

"So, it really is all about the café."

"That is where it started, but, if we are trying to come up with ideas, I suppose that we shouldn't limit the scope to the Unity." Léon regrets expressing his last thought.

"We should do something with the tables," Natalie suggests.

"Such as?" Eugenie asks.

"Put them outside."

"I like the idea; they seem to be just as important as the café and, unlike books and the like, we wouldn't need to have thousands of copies. Wouldn't the police just come and take them away, though?"

"Hervé would have to agree to have them left out in the elements," Léon adds.

"We don't use the originals then," Natalie counters.

The table falls into silence as the girls contemplate the possibilities and Léon considers the risks.

"How do we get our hands on coffee-house tables without raising suspicion?" Léon asks.

"Do they even have to be tables? It's only the tops that are unique," Eugenie wonders.

"What would we do with copies of the tops? Plaster them on the sides of buildings?"

"Wouldn't that need a ton of copies?"

Natalie listens to the flow of questions, waiting for it to taper off. Then she brings the conversation back to her original idea, albeit slightly modified. She is still taken by the experience of entering the Unity from the side door and making her way to where her father was sitting near the front. She was determined to convince her father to let her into his world of writing after having leafed through the journal he subsequently burned. Yet every table pulled at her; she found it impossible to directly approach her father.

"Let's focus on the tables. Okay, so we can't do all this ourselves, but we know where to find other tables – the Unity is not the only café in town – and I imagine that at least one of us knows people who can help with the rest. We should involve the least number of people possible though."

"As paradoxical as it might sound, we should also involve the least number of young people," Léon adds. He already has an idea of a place where he can find the tables and likely have them painted, but he keeps it to himself for the moment.

Eugenie nods, to her father's surprise: "We would already be taking a risk; there is no reason to add recklessness to the plan."

"Then we need a way to get the tables to where we want them to go and a way to keep them there," Natalie continues.

Léon has an idea for that too, and once again he is reluctant to express his thoughts. It seems to him that the girls are far enough from being able to put the plan in action that without his help they would not be able to do anything. It isn't the same sort of risk as them acquiring banned reading materials or fulfilling some youthful impulses to fight against the system, where they would have done something with or without him. At the same time, even though Natalie seems to be on an even keel, he knows that Eugenie needs some sort of pressure release. Beyond that, he feels somewhat beholden to Hervé, given how much Hervé has done for him over the years.

"And ideally we could do it all before the tables are returned," Natalie says.

"How can we copy them when they are in a warehouse somewhere?" Eugenie asks.

"I think that I know where the warehouse is. I have come across two with lots of black cars parked nearby. I went past them both after the tables were confiscated and one had more activity than usual."

"Did you actually see Hervé or the tables?"

"No, but it's worth a closer look."

"Even if they are there, how would we get in?"

"I'll figure something out."

Léon wants to say that it is a bad idea – particularly the part about rushing to make it happen while the tables are still in police hands – and that he wants no part of it. It would be wise to put an end to the planning before the girls get their hopes up.

Still, if this can be done without too much risk, perhaps he should support it. He would have to talk to some people to know for sure. At the very least, his position will seem more reasonable if he only says that it is a bad idea after a couple of conversations.

"I will make some inquiries," Léon offers, "on the condition that if it seems like there will be too much risk for whatever reason, we will pull the plug."

"So long as we decide that together," Eugenie says.

"Of course."

Eugenie divvies up the tasks, and then, realizing that she doesn't have much of a role at this point, asks what more she can do. Natalie and Léon are at a loss, which undermines Léon's motivation of providing her with an outlet. He briefly considers asking her if she would like to edit the newest issue of the journal, but dismisses it as that would leave far too much potentially illegal material at the house. In the end, they have to accept that they are not together due to complementary skills but simply because they are a family.

As soon as the necessary decisions are made, Léon heads back to the Metro to talk to Cesar. When he had come for the first time with Hervé, the spare tables stacked in a corner stuck out, due to their contrast with the practiced elegance of all the other aspects of the establishment. He also figures that, as the café is frequented by the artists Hervé once coveted, Cesar might point him in the direction of some regulars who could replicate the tables from the Unity. His reception is somewhat encouraging; instead of greeting him, or, more probably, Hervé, at the entrance, Cesar stays at his booth by the counter. That gives Léon an indication of how important Cesar considers Hervé.

Léon approaches the booth and Cesar invites him to sit. He explains a portion of the plan mixed with a dollop of fiction: "Essentially, we are concerned that one of these years, the government is going to decide to destroy the tables."

"The Committee is very big on forgetting; it is easier to instill their myths," Cesar says, nodding.

"We would like not only to record what is on them, but make a set of replicas. Last time we were in here, I noticed the tables in the corner of a café reputed for its talented artists and everything clicked when the Unity's tables were confiscated once again."

"Hervé's tables." Cesar shakes his head.

Léon, not quite sure if Cesar's gesture indicates that Hervé's tables are not worth replicating or that it would be a tragedy if they were lost, comes to his request: "Can we use your spare tables and the talent of some of your regulars?"

Cesar switches back to nodding: "I don't imagine that you intend to bring the originals here or think it proper to have my regulars go to the Unity. Do you have a camera?"

"The tables are in any case still in a government warehouse, so moving them would be a challenge. And we do not have a camera."

"I'll find you one," he continues to nod, but now at one of his customers, who takes the cue and comes to join them at the booth. "Thomas, an evening on the house – with the usual limits – for lending this gentleman your camera with some film, and developing the prints afterwards. Sound good?"

Thomas the performance artist grins and pulls a camera and some spare film from his bag. He gives Léon some quick instructions before handing him the camera and returning to his table. Léon, feeling awkward without a bag of his own, barely manages to stuff the equipment into his pockets. He stays for a drink, so as to not look suspicious to the police. Cesar regales him with tales of Hervé trying to convince and cajole a variety of artists to frequent the Unity, all the while turning a blind eye to the condescension of the poets who haunted his café at the time to creative types who didn't use words to express themselves. It is evident by the tone of Cesar's voice and his incessant nodding that he is very fond of Hervé. When Léon has finished his drink, he thanks his host and says that he will be back in a day or two.

Chapter 21

Lora is sitting on a pile of logs along the railroad track, beside a small platform and a large grain elevator, her bags at her feet. There is a steady breeze that slightly lessens the weight of the intense sun overhead. It was a relatively quick trip from Kralovna, only taking about an hour and a half. The train was rickety and the seats hard; despite a track that seemed perfectly flat and straight, she felt shaken up by the ride. Her fellow passengers were relatively noisy, talking about all sorts of serious subjects in a fairly light-hearted yet practical manner. The main topic was a new harvester that many of them had just seen for the first time in town, though the conversation quickly evolved into engines, parts, repairs, and onward. Since she left Kralovna she had been looking for reasons why her plan to become a backroom advisor was ultimately misguided. It struck her that always being constrained to stay quiet, to never speak her mind in the foreground, was a very good reason to consider herself better off now. She was seduced by Violet's shadowy ubiquity when Arria's brash courage made for a far better model, a sentiment easily expressed when she did not have much choice in the matter.

Before she left, an oversized envelope arrived from Léon. She had held on to it unopened until she felt that she might slip into overthinking her situation. The train ride was sufficiently distracting. The brief exploration of Los, a collection of houses and shops that she would consider more a hamlet than a town, was barely so. Sitting on the logs, waiting for the inspector, seems like an ideal time to see what her husband wants to show her. She goes through the packages and scribbled notes amused at how adventuresome dinners had become in the capital and reassured that at least some of her daughters' energy and imagination has been focused on such an innocent occupation. She is under no illusions that many other pursuits far less innocent – at least in the eyes of the Committee – were going on; they had however not completely taken over their lives.

The packages also make her hungry, so she goes back into the glorified town to get a bite to eat. When she wanders back, she notices a truck at the elevator and decides to take a closer look. The truck is backed into an enclosure connected to the several-stories-tall main structure. Two men are standing beside the enclosure, arguing over price. One of them, the elevator operator, is saying that the results from the sample of the wheat he had sent to the exchange in the capital for grading had come back with a number two grade. He explains heatedly, over the objections of the farmer, that it was impossible to have the result back from the capital in such a short time, and that the low grade was mainly due to kernel discolorations. The farmer is of course correct; even if his grain had fungal or bacterial issues there is no way that enough time had passed for it to have been properly tested. The operator suggests that, if the farmer does not believe him, he is free to take his grain elsewhere. The farmer protests for a while longer before finally accepting to unload his truck there.

While the operator starts up the bucket elevator, the farmer distances himself from the truck to avoid the dust cloud from the moving grain. Lora lets her curiosity get the better of her and asks him why he doesn't go to another elevator.

"He is the least corrupt operator around here," the farmer replies. "He is the only one that doesn't claim that the grain is less clean than normal and try to charge for it, nor does he short weigh the load. Heh, I thought you were going to ask why I was still selling grain a couple of months away from the next harvest."

"I didn't even think of that, but now that you mention it, why are you selling your grain so late?"

"It's a combination of having a great harvest last year and the railroad putting a low priority on agricultural shipments."

Lora nods knowingly; the decisions of the railway had such a significant impact on the yard and other aspects of the operations of her department that it is not surprising to find a similar situation here. "Would storing it for this long impact the grade?"

"Not if it is stored properly. And if there was a problem, it wouldn't have been the one the operator mentioned. Discoloration is a result of too much moisture when the kernel is still young."

"What did you do about the railway decision?" Lora asks, thinking that none of the farmers she knows – which is admittedly not very many – would sit still in such circumstances.

"Heh, we organize. Even when I was a kid, my parents would take me to meetings, and there are always new issues that crop up, but also opportunities. There are just too many things that we can't do by ourselves. Anyway, for this problem in particular we have put pressure on the government, with a predictably disappointing result, and have set our own quotas to make sure everyone survives. Don't get me wrong, we don't prop anyone up who is incapable of bringing their crop to harvest in an ordinary year and doesn't pull his weight when a road or clinic needs to be built. We just don't let people fail due to circumstances that are not under our control.

"My family has more land than most, so I have a bushel or two yet to sell beyond the quota."

"I heard it once said that prairie organizing was entrepreneurial socialism."

"Yeah, whatever. Call it what you like." The farmer, sensing a theoretical direction, glances back at the truck to see if it is empty.

"Does your area have telephones?" Lora asks, picking up on her misstep.

"Yeah, locally. We're not connected to the government system yet though."

"Are they useful?"

"You have no idea. It is so much easier to just pick up the phone than to have to go all the way to the next farm, especially if you don't know if they have what you need. I can't even imagine the number of times one of us needed a part or a tool or a cup of sugar and it was all arranged immediately. Setting up meetings and warning others of a change of operator at one of the elevators, all of it is so much easier now. But we can't reach the clinic in Los or anyone else beyond the loop. Hopefully that will change soon though; that," he points to the pile of poles, "is a start. Then all we need is for the wire to arrive and we should be good to go. I actually had a chance to use a phone at the post office with a properly energized copper line and it was amazing; I could use my normal voice and my wife – who was calling from Kralovna – could understand every word. I could even tell from the sound of her voice that it was her."

His excitement is cut off when the operator reappears and waves to him, indicating that all the grain has been unloaded. He turns back to Lora: "I take it that you are with the Department of Telephones?"

Lora nods.

"Well, maybe I will see you soon. I'm Nathan, by the way."

"Lora. Thank you for indulging my curiosity."

"My pleasure." Nathan walks back to the operator to finish the transaction while Lora returns to the stack of poles.

Fifteen minutes later, as Nathan is driving away, a car pulls up and a middle aged woman jumps out with surprising sprightliness.

"Lora?"

"Yes."

"Beatrix. These are your bags?"

"Yes."

Beatrix takes the bags and puts them in the back seat, motioning with her head for Lora to get in. Once both of them are installed, Beatrix starts driving down the bumpy, uneven road.

The shaking of the train that brought Lora to Los seems to her to have been pure luxury in comparison, as does the friendliness of Anna.

"Can I ask where we are going?" Lora asks, half an hour into the trip.

"I have one last stop, should be quick."

"Okay." She decides to hold off on asking questions along the lines of where she would be sleeping that night.

Another thirty minutes takes them to a pole that is evidently not up to standard, seemingly randomly placed beside the road. Beatrix hits the brakes to stare at it out her window before driving on, saying "very quick" under her breath. Lora looks up at the wire and sees what she thinks are barbs. She realizes that this is the impromptu style Anna described when she was explaining how she got started with telephones. Several poles and lengths of barbed wire further along, they come to a house with a mix of cars, tractors and horse-drawn carriages in front. Beatrix gets out of the car and takes several Development of Telephone guides for farmer syndicates from the back seat. Then she goes to the door, Lora following without any explicit direction.

The majority of the syndicate, about a dozen people in addition to the children in tow, is waiting for them in the kitchen, more or less around the table. They seem to have used every chair in the house, leaving a couple of younger members to lean against the counter. Beatrix pauses to look at the phone mounted on the wall in the front hallway before joining the group. A kitchen chair is left empty, which Beatrix takes. Lora leans against the wall behind her until one of the group, noticeably younger than her, offers her a chair and joins those leaning against the counter.

"Your loop is not up to standard," Beatrix says straight out, looking at each of the people facing her in turn. "It will not be connected to the department's system."

A couple of members look at each other, evidently unsure as to who should respond.

"I have brought you some guides so that you have some direction as to where to go from here," Beatrix continues. "The department also has advisors who can help you out. They can only advise though; they will not upgrade your loop for you."

A young man leaning against the counter decides to speak: "Can you go over what we need to improve?"

Beatrix briefly explains that the departmental system uses energized lines powered from the central exchange, which is the only way that calls can be carried over long distances. The lack of conductivity of barbed wire, coupled with incompatible phones, would practically mean that they would not be able to make or receive calls and, even if they did manage by some miracle to connect, neither person on each end of the line would be able to hear the other. Regarding the poles, it is clear that they are not seasoned and will quickly start to rot, for those that haven't already started. A connection to the network is useless if the lines are constantly down due to substandard poles. Basically, the department guarantees a high level of service within its network, but that requires that the syndicate upgrade the last mile to the level of the department's first hundred.

Lora feels bitter listening to Beatrix. She was instrumental in ensuring that the department's system – not just the lines but all the equipment – actually was at a high level when she was cut off at the knees. Phillip saw from almost the beginning that her background in the capital would be useful in negotiations between departments, yet he made no effort to keep her in that role. She knows that he made the right choice; the Committee would not have taken it well had he disregarded their order. Besides, after the order, she would have been persona non grata in the capital. Thinking about it just makes her feel more resentful.

She refocuses on the discussion and is surprised to find that the syndicate is taking Beatrix's explanation very well. She recognizes that Beatrix did concentrate on the practical aspects of the refusal. She was silent on the policies and directives of the department, except insofar as they had something to do with the department's portion of the system. Her point was simply that the syndicate's loop would not work with the department's network. From there the discussion, joined by several members of the group, aims to come up with practical solutions to rectify the loop's shortcomings.

Chapter 22

"Central asked me to come and take some pictures of the tabletops," Léon explains to the senior of the two inspectors having a cup of coffee with Hervé in the warehouse. Léon is thankful at this moment that the police force is large enough so that most agents don't recognize him or each other. "Apparently, one of the analysts wants to compare them with the papers of someone seen entering the Unified Café…"

"Unity Café," the inspector corrects him.

"Right, anyway, starts with a 'u'. He can't be bothered to come down here himself and since we can't very well send the tables to him, I'm here to take some photos." Léon almost says that he could come back at lunchtime so as to not disrupt the interrogation before realizing that an inspector would not willingly spend his lunch working.

The inspector looks vaguely suspicious, but finds the distraction welcome. He looked at Hervé's file before talking to him, so he knows that bringing him in is just done for form and that nobody gets anything interesting out of the interrogations. Maybe if he was ten years younger he would be more ambitious and try to succeed where others had failed. As it stands, he prefers just going through the motions and making the point clear that Hervé should keep his nose as clean as possible, given that he runs an underground café, since the police can intervene at any time. The point could be made in a morning though, so he has become increasingly listless as the days have passed.

"Fine," the inspector replies, showing Léon to where the tables are kept.

Léon starts snapping the photos, trying to keep as steady as possible. He can't believe that he is doing this; every fiber of his body tells him to get out, yet he knows that if he tries to run, his nervousness will make him trip over his feet and land on his face, probably upending a table or two in the process. Luckily, the inspector goes back to the dinosaur/bird table where Hervé is in the middle of giving a nonsensical explanation of the struthiomimus poem to his partner. Léon hears a slight pause in Hervé's story, likely because Hervé recognizes him, but he is too scared that looking at his friend will betray them both to find out.

Yesterday, with the tacit acceptance of Hervé the laundryman, Natalie brought home a couple of police uniforms. Following her drive to experience more of life, her plan was for her and Léon to simply knock on the door of the warehouse. Eugenie nixed the idea, saying that Natalie was too young to pull it off, and then suggested herself. Léon then stepped into the trap of insisting that he would only do it alone, that he could not accept his daughters taking such risks. They then reluctantly agreed on the condition that they would accompany him to the warehouse, which had to happen in any case as he had no idea where it was. He added one more condition; that the search for the warehouse was timed so that as soon as they found it, the girls would be able to head to school immediately after and arrive on time.

The correct warehouse turned out to be the second, less active one, which made sense in retrospect. It was not as if Hervé was a high profile target that needed a great deal of manpower. Léon modified Natalie's route to the two sites slightly in order to pass by the transit authority and have a couple of words with Etienne before Etienne started his shift. As Léon expected, but did not exactly hope, it did not take much convincing for him, with his van and tools, to come on board for the second phase, assuming that that first phase was successful. To Léon's way of thinking, Etienne had always been a bit overenthusiastic when it came to anything considered to be shenanigans. Other than that, he was perfect for the job.

When they arrived at the first warehouse, a freshly unloaded truck was just pulling out from the loading dock, giving a clear view of a limited portion of the inside. There were rows upon rows of racks containing all sorts of packages. A couple of black cars then showed up. Inspectors entered and, several minutes later, exited with boxes too small to be tables. Though it was not definitive, the three decided to give the second warehouse a try. Their timing turned out to be perfect, since they caught a glimpse of Hervé entering the building accompanied by two inspectors as soon as they showed up. They then ducked into an alley so that Léon could take off his loose fitting clothes to expose the uniform underneath. Natalie hugged her father excitedly while Eugenie kept her distance, simply wishing him good luck, before they left him to enter the warehouse alone. As soon as his daughters had left, Léon started shaking and had to lean against a wall to avoid collapsing. He found himself once more thinking about Lora's letter where she described them both as courageous and once more wondering how anyone could think that he was strong. He nonetheless tried to convince himself that she was right as he managed to stand on his own two feet and found himself walking towards the main door Hervé and the inspectors used not long before.

Léon progresses slowly, unfamiliar with Thomas's camera and worried that the pictures will come out blurry. This anxiety keeps his fear of being in the lion's den in check until the inspector he spoke to at the door decides that his photographs are worthier of his attention than the interminable nonsense that Hervé spouts to ridicule the questions he is asked year after year. The inspector starts by looking over his shoulder, but soon starts asking questions about the film Léon is using and the settings of the camera. Léon thinks that the questions are just part of the inspector's default setting when he is at work in an effort to reassure himself. The idea that he is only being interrogated by habit is however not very comforting, making it more and more difficult for him not to start shaking again.

"What is your opinion of the Contax?" the interrogator asks, referring to the camera.

Léon has to bite back his automatic response of 'I refuse to testify', leaving his mind completely blank. He continues to move between the tables, taking photos. Luckily, the inspector views the lack of response more as a result of Léon's focus on his task than anything untoward.

"I am thinking about getting one myself," he continues in a low enough voice to not be heard by Hervé and the other inspector. "The botanical garden has a collection of orchids that I would love to take pictures of."

Léon is taken aback by this glimpse of humanity, the first that he had seen in an inspector. His mind starts sketching out a new feuilleton, which puts him more at ease. An interesting continuation of the story would be if the inspector started taking the pictures for him, so he goes with it.

"Do you want to try the camera, take some of the photos?" Léon asks. "I confess to not being very interested or knowledgeable in the subject; I just borrowed it from someone else at central."

"I would love to give it a try," the inspector says, somewhat louder and more enthusiastically than appropriate with an interrogation going on across the room.

Léon hands over the camera and starts giving the instructions that Thomas had offered him. The inspector just nods distractedly and moves to the next table. It becomes clear a moment later that, while he might not be familiar with this particular model, he is well-versed in the technology in general. It is also evident that Léon's mind is not quite at ease as he initially thought and that without the distraction of the camera his self-consciousness is almost overwhelming. He doesn't even know how inspectors typically stand, let alone interact with the world. His stance might be too stiff or too casual; the inspector might look up in a moment and know instantly that he is not who he says he is. The habit of letting his mind wander to neutralize his emotions just makes him feel more out of place as an inspector.

"I haven't been to the botanical gardens for years," Léon says in an effort to distract himself from his anxiety. "I don't remember the orchids specifically, but I recall thinking that some of the flowers were just stunning, so full of life and energy in such a peaceful setting."

"That was awfully poetic," the inspector says, glancing up. Léon's anxiety spikes, but the inspector is already bringing his eye to the viewfinder for another shot. "You should go back; it has been significantly expanded in the past couple of years, ever since the Committee made it a priority. When you were there, the orchid collection was probably just a couple of plants."

The inspector takes his time with the photos, conscious of the framing and composition. As he becomes more familiar with the camera and the best technique to shoot tables in the space, his pace picks up. The second inspector continues to guide Hervé around to answer questions for each poem at each table. Despite having already covered the majority of tables on previous days, he manages to find a route that avoids contact between Hervé and the camera. An hour later, the inspector is giving Léon his contact information and asking to be informed when the film has been developed so he can take a look. He likes the camera and is already acquainted with the film and the work of the darkroom technicians at central, where he assumes Léon will take the roll, so the only question that remains is the quality of the end result.

A couple of minutes later, Léon finds himself outside, walking to the alley where he had left his clothes. The walk is if anything more difficult than when he was going to the warehouse. The tension that kept him upright and still through the experience melts away, leaving him drained and faltering. In his imagination, he saw himself elated and full of energy from putting one over on the police. Instead, even the incessant inner voice that needles him whenever he takes foolish risks no longer has the force to nag him. He wants to find a corner to collapse in, but satisfies himself with finding a relatively clean spot in the alley to sit down for a moment, once the uniform is covered up.

That afternoon, he returns to the Metro. Not seeing Thomas the performance artist, he heads directly to Cesar's booth and puts the camera on the table.

"Hervé will start to think that I am poaching his regulars," Cesar says, nodding. "Tomorrow, end of the day, the tables should be done. How are you going to pick them up?"

"I have a van lined up."

"Loading them won't be subtle. I get my deliveries early in the morning, from five to seven, and the police don't usually show up until after that. You should come then."

Léon nods and orders a drink.

"You look spent," Cesar observes, shaking his head.

"Stressful morning," Léon replies without elaborating.

"Successful, though?"

"Yes, I suppose it was." Léon wants to add 'But to what end?' but can't imagine that such a question would do much to motivate Cesar to continue helping him. Instead, he asks, "How did you and Hervé get to know each other?"

"We were servers together a very long time ago, at the restaurant in the Hotel of Peace. A very high class establishment, lots of clients from all over the world, shut down later because the owners were suspected of inappropriate foreign sympathies. During the protests leading up to the installation of the current Committee, we bled in the street together. We weren't even protesting, just making our way to the train station for the restaurant's sideline of selling prepared food to travelers."

Cesar describes the time with affection, when the whole city seemed to be bursting with youthful vitality, before the energy was sucked out by the Committee's obsession with normalcy.

Chapter 23

Lora crisscrosses the countryside with Beatrix. The inspections take two basic forms; if the loop is obviously substandard, they just speak with the syndicate and point them in the right direction; if the loop looks good they verify and test all the components. To Lora's relief, climbing poles is unnecessary most of the time, since they can, more often than not, test the wire where it enters the houses. It is only when they have to pinpoint a fault in an otherwise good line that climbing is required. For the first two inspections, Lora just follows along, but after that she takes some initiative. Beatrix only gives Lora direction when she is doing something wrong, which doesn't give Lora much insight into what she is supposed to be doing. When they are in the car, she has taken to reading the guide that Beatrix gives out to syndicates, and, when they are on-site, she generally takes care of the tasks that do not deal with the line, such as testing the poles and verifying that the phones capable of handling centrally energized lines are in place. This split in labor quickly becomes routine with minimum communication. Lora knows that at some point she will have to push Beatrix to show her how to do more but is in no hurry to do that.

Official accommodations have been arranged for the most part in rooming houses and exchange buildings. As Lora learns the first night, inspectors also take advantage of the hospitality of the farmer syndicates, especially when the loop is quite far from a town and the inspection is late in the day. She is uncomfortable with the obvious conflict this seems to create, but, lacking any reasonable alternative, she keeps such thoughts to herself and follows Beatrix's lead. It helps that in the culture out here, propriety takes a backseat to practicality. That does not make being in such close proximity to a family in the privacy of their home any easier for her.

After her experience in Kralovna, she does find it easier to adapt, though she is increasingly convinced that it will never be possible for her to fully adopt the pragmatic culture. She can't bring herself to focus herself entirely on concrete issues, just as she was incapable of simply working in the yard when so much more was at least hypothetically possible. Perhaps the life of a farmer, particularly a wheat farmer whose livelihood is so precarious, would preclude thinking about lofty goals, but she doesn't think so. With farming technology improving all the time, the horizon is far more open now than it has ever been. Anna's family is a case in point; even on the farm, Anna was able to spend more time working on the local telephone loop than farming and her older brother could have left the farm to go to university, had Committee policies not stood in his way. Anna is not perfectly happy working in the yard, but she will continue to do so for essentially practical reasons, in order for her family to conform to Committee expectations so that her younger siblings can go to university. The goals have moved beyond the farm and are not all that different than Lora's own desire to keep the door to higher education open for her daughters. Anna could do more for herself at the risk of being impractical, just as Lora could keep her head down and avoid all risks, but neither is inclined to do that.

One evening marks an exception to accommodation rules, as the final inspection of the day is for an impeccable loop constructed by the syndicate of her train acquaintance, Claude. Despite the weight loss and weathering that have accompanied the transition from sitting indoors all day to working outside, Claude recognizes her before she is able to place him and introduces her to his family and the group as an old friend. After the inspection is finished and the results are presented to representatives of the syndicate, he invites her to stay the night and, even though a town with official rooms available is a short distance away, she is inclined to accept. Once he promises to have her in town first thing in the morning, Beatrix shrugs and drives off. The rest of the group lingers to congratulate themselves and offer preliminary suggestions for their next project. Claude's family, including his wife and an adult son and daughter, act as hosts, serving light refreshments. Lora does not participate in the conversation and nobody seems to notice or care.

When the guests have gone, the family cleans up and starts making a late dinner. Lora sits at the kitchen table to be closer to the activity, and finds herself in the strange position of being in such an intimate space and yet feeling completely alien to the concert playing out in front of her. She recognizes that this is Léon's typical position and tries to imagine how he has felt over the years being more an observer of than a participant in his own family. She can't envision it, but then she has trouble seeing how he can regularly chronicle his life as a disgraced writer. She could barely stand the distance she felt between her and her daughters when she last visited the capital. The irony is that the remoteness of both her and Léon are for practical reasons, yet the consequences of living with a father who is present but not available and having a mother leave during a trying point in their lives cannot be healthy for Eugenie and Natalie. The choices were certainly practical on a certain level, but nonsensical on another.

Claude extricates himself from the food preparation as soon as he is able and joins his guest at the table with an aperitif and a handful of glasses. He pours five, hands one to Lora and toasts her presence.

"So, you have managed not only to survive the provincial town but also the open prairie. I'm impressed."

"You and me both," Lora replies, taking a sip. "And I was under the impression that you thought telephones were a luxury."

"Well, as you have undoubtedly come to realize, we are not inclined to spend time on things that we cannot change. Railroads are still our biggest problem, but we haven't gotten much traction in changing them. At least with telephones, we can coordinate better amongst ourselves, which is nothing to sneeze at. As you probably overheard when the group was throwing around ideas for future projects, we are going to start taking control of elevators soon. Since they are single purpose, we are not finding the same resistance from the government as with the railroads."

"Soon you will be taking over the world."

"That doesn't sound like the woman I met on the train not so long ago, with that fresh-from-the-capital sheen."

"It is hard to keep that sheen when I am forced to use the roads you have out here. I thought you said that they were decent."

"It is all part of our nefarious plan to keep the Committee thugs from our doorstep. In fact, over the years, we have never seen your famous black cars and only one highly polished bureaucrat has graced us with her presence."

"Her name wouldn't have been Violet, would it?" Lora asks, half joking.

"As it happens, yes. Very pleasant and polite, but it was never clear why she was here."

"She didn't ask about me?" Lora suddenly wonders if her fate was sealed long before her work for Phillip.

"Not that I recall. She was interested in the barriers to success grain farmers faced and that was about it. Oh, and we also talked about hockey; she was quite a fan. Do you know her?"

"I have come to be of the opinion that nobody really knows her, but we have crossed paths once or twice."

"Ah. Anyway, besides the roads, how have you found things out here?"

"A lot less constrained than in the capital, that's for sure. It seems like the Committee isn't quite sure how to deal with realities out here. It isn't just the farmers either; the Department of Telephones has a lot of independence. And I have rarely seen a single black car in Kralovna, let alone the three that the police typically use for surveillance in the capital. On the other hand, it is difficult to move anything forward without buy-in from the capital. The railways are a great example of one of the points of centralized control, but it does not stop there. Have your kids thought about going to university?"

"Briefly, but there is lots of work to do on the farm. That sort of thing comes up more in families with four or more kids. Does this mean that you tried to move a project forward and got slapped down?"

"No, I helped move something forward in my department and it was a success, but only with the involvement of other, more centralized departments." Lora feels that she can be very open with Claude, but is still not about to admit to how she ended up as an inspector.

"To be honest, one of the reasons we did not explore the idea of university further is that we know of too many families that have been unsuccessful because they are landowners and the value of the land and the farming equipment is quite high. That seems to blind the Committee to the fact that we live off our labor; we don't lease the land to other people and sit idle while the money pours in. Nor are we agitators for private property right; even if we believe in them, we have far more pressing issues for the foreseeable future."

The food needs some time to cook, so the rest of the family joins Claude and Lora at the table for their aperitif.

"You aren't talking about anything too serious, I hope," Ursula, Claude's wife says.

"Not at all," Claude replies, "we are just chatting about the differences between the capital, where Lora is from, and our humble farm. There are evidently a great many."

Claude's wife and children follow his implied suggestion and ask Lora a series of questions about her experiences in the capital. She responds superficially, as if she was giving advice to tourists.

They had been there several times and had taken advantage of the officially sanctioned diversions, of which there were many, and did not really notice what was going on in the background. They found the locals pleasant but terse, unwilling to venture very far into a given subject. They assumed that this was typical for a larger city, which is certainly correct to a certain extent.

Once the food has been served, the conversation shifts to the current projects of Rose and Paul, the daughter and son. Rose is trying to bring an old tractor back from the dead. She had ordered some parts from a supplier and had just received a package containing a note stating that the country was out of what she was looking for and some random parts so she wouldn't be empty handed. The family has a laugh about the odd turn of phrase and does not seem surprised by this result. They apparently have a garage full of random parts, some of which end up coming in handy some time later. Lora recounts in turn her experience with the rubber boots and headlamps at the Department of Telephones' store. Paul brings up his successes in cultivating squash that reaches a significant size before the seeds harden, a feat that, given the family's supportive reaction, he has been working towards for a while.

The cohesion of Claude's family is evident. Claude and Ursula support and encourage their children insofar as possible, given their place in the system. After dinner, Lora asks Claude and Ursula their advice; is it better to ensure that one's children have the widest range of opportunities available at the cost of being a hypocritical role model or close off certain opportunities by being forthright about and acting on what one believes is actually important. The advice given is ambiguous, but it doesn't matter since Lora has already made a decision in regards to her daughters. She knows from her visit to the capital that they cannot live full lives within the Committee's precepts and she doesn't want them to follow her lead, either in the sense of conforming to the government's expectations of normalcy or trying to become the flawless mechanical woman.

The next morning, Lora asks Beatrix for a couple of days off and heads back to the capital.

Chapter 24

The last table Etienne bolted to the sidewalk was removed six hours after it was installed. The police, notified that a transit authority van was seen close to the location of the table at about the time it was installed, invited the entire maintenance staff for a cup of coffee at central. Everyone questioned repeated the story of the acquisition of vans too large for their bays, concluding that since the vans had to be left outside all the time, anyone could have borrowed one. The transit authority supervisor who was in place since the scandal of the van purchases was reassigned and that avenue of the investigation was closed. The first act of the new supervisor was to have the bay entrances enlarged.

Hervé, whose questioning had come to an end a day before the tables appeared on sidewalks around the city, was fingered internally by the police as the mastermind. He had been under constant surveillance since the original tables had been confiscated however, so it was decided that it would be too much of an embarrassment to accuse him publicly and admit that the inspectors watching him had missed something so significant. The idea was floated to send him to prison on an unrelated charge, but it was deemed more important to keep the Unity running and all the regulars in one place. Unfortunately, he was so busy with reopening the café that he did not notice a table that managed to survive four hours a block up the street, nor the commotion when the police came to remove it.

Cesar's coffee schedule was moved up, due to visits to the Metro by Hervé and a Unity regular, Léon, in the lead up to the table incident. Since the tables at the Metro had not been considered to be of interest in the past, inspectors had not noted the stack in reports from previous searches of the café and nobody noticed that it was missing this time around.

Unlike Hervé, Cesar hires sufficient staff in order for him to be able to stay in his booth, from which he can survey the entirety of his domain. He trusts his staff enough to let them run the café in his absence, so the inspectors in the black cars across the street did not get a break while he was answering questions at central.

For the Chaulieu family, the whole experience was like a dream. None of them had a chance to see the tables in the daytime and they had no idea if anyone else even noticed them, let alone if they made a lasting impression. Given the habit of people in the capital to tuck their head between their shoulders and avoid noticing anything that could complicate their lives, there was good reason to be pessimistic about the effectiveness of the plan. Of course, this same habit made it impossible for the police to find witnesses who could describe the people responsible for installing the tables, which balanced things out somewhat. Léon explained to his daughters that that was how his journal, and many other underground creative works, was received; once he put an issue out in the world, he had very little idea where it would end up and the path it took to get there, nor did he have an accurate sense of who was actually reading it and who was just passing it on or destroying it. Besides the regulars at Unity, the only people who ever openly talk to him about it are the inspectors with whom he has a cup of coffee from time to time.

The dream was nonetheless very agreeable for both Eugenie and Natalie. Léon was of course hesitant to include his daughters in the second phase of the plan, but knew both that it was not his choice to make and that there was little chance that his daughters would accept being completely excluded from a plan that they had for the most part come up with in the beginning. Besides, the extra hands for loading and unloading the tables were welcome since nobody wanted to stay at any one location any longer than absolutely necessary. Regardless of a result that could only be considered disappointing compared to what they had imagined – the tables up for months, with thousands and thousands of people passing by and reading the poems, eventually making them both an institution and a legend – they were out there doing something that they believed in.

The experience also had a sublime poetry that Natalie in particular appreciated. The work started in the darkness before dawn. They loaded the tables under a black sky, with the glow from the city and dispersed altocumulus clouds hiding the stars. As they installed them, the sky transformed from a vague grey to a fiery red, reflected on the lacquered surface of the last few tables. During the installation, there were moments when she paused to take in what was around her, lost in the moment. Eugenie, who was in any case keeping an eye on her, had to nudge her a couple of times to bring her back to the task at hand. After her fixation on the poetry of the imperfect and the ordinary, this was a revelation, the consequences of which have yet to emerge.

Once Eugenie was aware that the tables had been removed, she decided to put the plan in the same column as the school newspaper; not a lasting success, but enough to treat as a learning experience. The end of her final school year was fast approaching though, which, added to the anxiety of whether she would get into university or not, was enough of a distraction to put formulating new plans on hold for the time being. The installation of the tables was however quite different than the newspaper in ways that have had a durable influence on how she sees herself, even though she may have not fully realized it. The newspaper was a product of the high school microcosm, with the drama playing out almost entirely in that environment. In espousing Hervé's more universal ideals, she was able to break from viewing her classmates and teachers as central players in her world. Had she followed Albert's lead when he took a step back from the newspaper to focus on bigger projects, she would have likely made the transition sooner. She would have also had to make a complete and likely irreversible break with school and all aspects – positive and negative – of normalcy.

Léon is back in the Unity at the original fungus table, typing out copies of the new issue of the journal. Hervé brings a new pot of lemon tea and joins him.

"Have I ever mentioned that I am flattered to have inspired your table adventure," Hervé says.

Léon nods without looking up, having heard this already numerous times.

"What do you have planned next?"

Léon shakes his head, feeling vaguely like Cesar.

"You are going to just continue doing what you have always done?"

"Not true," Léon replies, knowing that if he keeps typing with Hervé at the table, he will make too many errors. "Your dear inspector has inspired me to visit our botanical gardens, which are really very pleasant. The flowers you see do not incessantly natter at me to take risks I am not comfortable taking."

"I would expect nothing more from you; I just keep hoping that one of your lovely and talented daughters will drag you into something interesting."

"They have inspired me to shift my writing to include more opinion and less description, though I am still unsure as to whether that is an improvement."

"I'm fairly sure that nobody will notice; your daily life is an opinion in itself."

"The opinion that one should not follow the rules to the letter but not rock the boat either, I suppose."

"Perhaps so. I imagine that one of the reasons the police did not look at you more closely when they were investigating the table adventure is that, after so many years of subverting the rules in a safe and predictable way, they couldn't imagine that you would do something so brazen."

"That's likely part of it. I have it on good authority that inspectors do not like having a cup of coffee with me because they know that I will write about it afterwards. They hate the idea of having an independent record of the interrogation out in the world, as it undermines their control of the situation and could prove to be embarrassing later on. You know that I regularly send a courtesy copy of the feuilleton to them; my way of saying thanks for giving me something to write about."

"You have mentioned it on occasion, and that supports my point. Given your history and habits, you could do more without much of an increase in the possibility that they will lock you up."

"Given recent history, I think that it is prudent to save up my get out of jail free cards for family use. Imagine if I had taken your advice and risked more before the table adventure, as you enjoy calling it. On the bright side for you, there is a very good chance that future harebrained schemes will aim to close the generational gap and make banned and underground culture more accessible. I doubt that they will succeed in any great measure, but that's neither here nor there. Bugging me will not help your cause though; you just have to be patient and leave me to my journal."

"Yes, yes I should," Hervé says without moving. "While you were absorbed by your adventure, the charter was written."

"The charter?"

"We discussed it the last time you graced us with your presence in the evening."

"Right," Léon responds; Lora's visit seems like a lifetime ago.

"You should sign it."

"What does it say?"

"It basically reminds the Committee of their obligations under the constitution, as well as international agreements to which the country is signatory, points out where the government has fallen short and demands that these shortcomings are corrected. You should of course read it before you sign."

"Right. I don't think that what I have been saying has had much of an impact."

"Of course it has. You won't initiate any adventures so I should stop bugging you about it."

"You do realize the risk of putting my name on a document like that. It would be like painting a target on my back. I'm not sure why we are even discussing this."

"Like it or not, you are a part of our little community. That is a major reason why you can go to bookish Thomas, Cesar and Etienne for help with your projects. Others have tried to follow the lead of people like you and Lucien, pursuing their art without making too many waves, and are now in prison. Keeping your head down is working for you for the moment, but for how much longer? What will happen when Natalie asks for more books, perhaps ones from abroad, and nobody is left to help you get them? Several members of the usual group that contributes to and reads your journal are gone; what will you do when they are all locked up?"

"And signing the charter will change that?"

"Probably not, but at least we won't be skulking around in the dark waiting for something to happen."

"And your legacy?"

"I'm in the same boat. If everyone is in prison, the Unity is dead."

"I will read the charter, but cannot promise anything more."

"You will have it tomorrow."

Léon struggles to get through the copy he is in the middle of typing, and then gives up for the day, his mood having been shaken by Hervé's words. He sips his tea and reflects on the charter. He can't see why his signature would be important; he may be reasonably well known in the community, insofar as there even is a community, but he is almost completely unknown outside of it. If only he signed it right after his books were banned, when his work was still well known. Then again, as someone who can't publish officially, can't hold a job and is already under regular surveillance, he has far less to lose than a guild writer with a clean record. The only thing he has left from his previous life is his family. The plan he and Lora agreed to before she left for Kralovna is in rough shape, but there is a chance that their daughters still have an open future.

Chapter 25

Lora and Léon are sitting at the kitchen table in silence. Lora arrived late last night. Léon did not realize that she was beside him until this morning. They both sat at the table while Eugenie and Natalie got ready for school. With less than a week to go, the girls were especially preoccupied and didn't register much surprise at finding their mother at home. Once the resonance of the banged door and brief 'bye dad', 'bye mom' had died down, Lora explained why she was back in the capital. She concluded that it no longer made sense – perhaps it never made sense – to use their children as the central reason to lead such perverse lives. This was such a significant change in how she approached problems that Léon was at a loss for words. She had always been so calculating; she had figured out how to balance Léon's record and ongoing writing with the rest of the family so that the police would not regularly show up at the house and interfere with the girls' schooling, she gauged exactly when she had to leave the judiciary so that she herself was not put on trial, etc., etc. On the other hand, now that the girls are privy to most of what they had hidden from them, perhaps it was better to not actively encourage living a lie.

Léon cannot decide what he thinks is best. Instead, he walks over to his jacket and pulls out his notebook, from which he takes several loose pages tucked in at the back. He comes back to the table and explains that this is the charter he had mentioned when she was last in the capital. She remembers the discussion straight away, giving him the impression that she had thought about it far more than he had. He then works forward from the visit, recounting how the family's situation had evolved. It is Lora's turn to be at a loss, never imagining that he would take the risk of impersonating an inspector or holding a café table steady while it is being bolted into a public, completely exposed sidewalk.

The silence passes as they read over and discuss the charter together. Hervé had described it accurately and they agree with all the points. When they reach the end, Lora asks no one in particular what they should do. Léon, while conceding Lora's conclusion about the destructiveness of leading false lives, just as he had Hervé's about the decimation of the community, believes that it is best to do nothing. The situation has already changed between them and the girls, so there is no need to take any drastic action. He then tries to take the conversation away from the charter by suggesting that she should try to find a job back in the capital, regardless of any increased risk. Lora smiles sadly at this, knowing that the Committee will not accept her coming back anytime soon. Léon, seeing that his attempt did not work and regretting that he brought the charter to the table to begin with, suggests that they wait until the girls come home and discuss it as a family before making any decisions.

"Does the charter reflect the sort of society we want for both ourselves and our children?" Lora asks directly.

"Yes, there's no denying that, but…"

Lora takes a pen from her bag and signs the document. Then she looks Léon in the eyes while pushing both to his side of the table: "Léon, it does not hurt."

Léon swallows, takes the pen, and signs. He tucks it back into his notebook and heads to the Unity to give it back to Hervé. Hervé pours him a drink, which he swallows in one gulp before leaving without a word. He takes a circuitous route back. If he was Paetus, nothing would matter anymore. By the time he reaches his front door, he decides that that is a good philosophy to have; he all but signed a confession, so now all there is to do is to wait for the verdict.

He enters and joins Lora, who has in the meantime moved to the living room. After deciding to tell the girls about the charter after Natalie comes home from work, Lora entertains her husband with tales of her short time as an inspector. Eugenie arrives a short time later, looking happy yet perplexed.

"I was called into the principal's office today, which was weird because the only time that had ever happened before was when they told me that they were shutting down the newspaper. So I went, and he announced that I had been accepted at the university. It was great news, but really weird since everyone else just got letters. There was a woman I had never seen before sitting silently at the back of the office, which made it even stranger. As I was leaving, she finally spoke, asking me to tell you, mom, that Maurice is playing piano again, whatever that means."

**TOP HAT
BOOKS**

Historical fiction that lives.

We publish fiction that captures the contrasts, the achievements, the optimism and the radicalism of ordinary and extraordinary times across the world.

We're open to all time periods and we strive to go beyond the narrow, foggy slums of Victorian London. Where are the tales of the people of fifteenth century Australasia? The stories of eighth century India? The voices from Africa, Arabia, cities and forests, deserts and towns? Our books thrill, excite, delight and inspire.

The genres will be broad but clear. Whether we're publishing romance, thrillers, crime, or something else entirely, the unifying themes are timescale and enthusiasm. These books will be a celebration of the chaotic power of the human spirit in difficult times. The reader, when they finish, will snap the book closed with a satisfied smile.